Praise for the Book

"How to convert adverse situations into opportunities for the bank is very lucidly written by Mr Gokhale in various episodes. The anecdotes narrated and the tips given by him at the end of each episode as 'Take Away' would be found quite useful by practicing bankers."

Rajeev Rishi
Chairman and Managing Director,
Central Bank of India

———

Shri Waman Gokhale, who retired as Deputy General Manager of Central Bank of India after over 40+ years of service, has brought out this publication aimed at branch bankers. He has explained the lessons learnt in banking from various anecdotes drawn from his career. Learning based on such anecdotes, in my view, is an extension of our 'Karma Parampara' tradition and effective considering the target audience of this book. The book conveys what needs to be conveyed to a banker at a branch or at the controlling office seeking to enhance the overall efficiency of his / her branch. It addresses different dimensions of branch banking – Customer service, operations and internal housekeeping, branch management, etc.

I am sure that this book will be useful to bankers and is an addition to the library on practical banking.

S. Sridhar
Former Chairman and Managing Director
Central Bank of India and National Housing Bank

BANKING

BEYOND

BOOKS

Stories of a Successful Banker

BANKING
BEYOND
BOOKS

Stories of a Successful Banker

WAMAN GOKHALE

Diamond Publications

BANKING BEYOND BOOKS
Waman Gokhale

First Edition : November, 2015

ISBN 978-81-8483-649-3

© Diamond Publications

Cover Page :
Sham Bhalekar

Published by :
Diamond Publications
264/3 Shaniwar Peth, 302 Anugrah Apartment
Near Omkareshwar Temple, Pune - 411 030
☎ 020-24452387, 24466642

info@diamondbookspune.com
www.diamondbookspune.com

Sole Distributor :
Diamond Book Depot
661 Narayan Peth
Appa Balwant Chowk
Pune 411 030
Tel. - 24480677, 66020282

Foreword

Perhaps this is the second occasion that I am writing the foreword of the book written by Mr. Waman Gokhale, on his banking experience of over 40 years and I assure you that I am equally fascinated to do so. His first book was 'A Kit on Documentation', which was in respect of credit facilities sanctioned by banks and was for internal use of the organization, Central Bank of India. That book is still being very actively used as a 'Bible' by staff at 4700+ branches of Central Bank of India. The present book, **'Banking Beyond Books,'** unfolds in a story- telling mode the important aspect of Human relationship in banking and how to apply various Managerial skills on the job. The real life stories are very enchanting and have strength to continuously keep the reader spellbound. Every story is different from the other and is a kaleidoscope showing the various situations faced by a banker. The chapter on 'Customers' gives insight how to create a bridge of confidence between a banker and its customers, so as to wow! the customers. The various incidences written in the book on difficult situations and difficult customers, gives incite to the bankers, how to handle such situations successfully as well how an adversity can be converted into opportunity. The chapter on 'Social Engineering' reflects how a Banker while working can play a vital role of helping the society. The story, Unity in Diversity, is a good example of social engineering. The deft handling of extremely difficult situation of loss of 81 cheques is a real stunner. The author has shown how through planned efforts and team work the collection of 81 duplicate cheques was achieved in the record time of three months and that too without any loss. In fact the adverse situation was leveraged to develop new relations resulting into the growth of business for the branch. As the Chairman and

Managing Director of the bank, I was a close observer of the event of renovation of '**Monumental Heritage Building' of Mumbai Main Branch during the Centenary Year 2010-2011.** The stupendous task was carried out very efficiently by the team headed by Mr. Gokhale. His knack of dealing with the people and societal centricity, along with his ability to converge with opposites could make him successful.

The various episodes reflect how through the team work the difficulties can be over ridden and converted into opportunities. The author has shown through his example how the edifice of any successful banking business stands on the pedestal of interpersonal relations and trust.

Mr. Gokhale has proved that the knowledge and the skills acquired during his career as a faculty can be very effectively applied on the job. He had in real sense walked a talk. The **Take Away** at the end of each story is a real value addition to the book, as they are the tips for the practical applications of various soft skills required for everyday management.

I can assure the readers that this book would be a great addition in understanding the soft skills and would be very useful guide even to the generation 'y', while fulfilling their managerial responsibilities. From an academic point of view, this book is a treasure trove of attributes: attitude, humility, behavior, and empowering style those are necessary to become a successful leader.

The author has humbly and very rightly given all the credit of his success to his colleagues, management, customers and to his great Institution.

I congratulate Mr. Gokhale for his excellent Book, on his Banking Experiences and I am sure that it will be very well received by the Banking fraternity, management students and the readers in general who would gain by addition to their knowledge bank.

Mohan Tanksale,
Chief Executive, Indian Banks Association and
Ex. Chairman and Managing Director, Central Bank Of India.

Preface

I have an immense pleasure to present my 40+ years of banking experience in a book form. It includes the days while working with Central Bank of India, one of the apex Public Sector Banks. I dedicate this book to my beloved late Mother and Father, but for their continuous encouragement a humble person like me who Joined Bank as a clerk could rise to the post of Deputy General Manager. Of Course, I am extremely thankful to my Branch Managers, Officers, Executives; Colleagues and Subordinates who had a great share in my making. My esteemed Institution Central Bank of India has given me all the opportunities one can get in his career. **I was bestowed with a rare honour to be a Branch Manager of the glamorous Mumbai Main Office the fountain head of the Bank and that too during 'The Centenary Year of The Bank'. At the same, I feel very proud while telling you that I had a very rare opportunity to occupy the very Chair, Table and the Cabin once adorned by our beloved founder, Sir Sorabji Pochkhanawala.** I was the last Branch Manager who got this life time reward from the Bank Management and I have no words to express my gratitude for this recognition. We have a wonderful array of customers of all creed and caste, rich, middle class and poor spread across the length and breadth of the country, who extended their unstinted support throughout my career and hence I could become a successful banker. Similarly I must thank the leaders of all the unions for their positive support .I will fail in my duties if I do not mention the name of my loving wife Mrs. Smita who had very ably handled all the family responsibilities as I was away from the family for quite a long period. It is because of her I could pay my full attention towards the banking career. My daughter, son as well as brother and sisters also had their silent contribution. The preface will be incomplete without mention of two of my wonderful colleagues who joined the bank along with me more or less at the same time in 1972-1973. I was the junior most in the branch, a direct recruit straight from The Institute of Science, not knowing even A, B, C of banking. My friend Shri Hemant, a Gold Medalist, Post Graduate student of Commerce had an uncanny art of teaching. He taught me right from fundamentals of double entry book keeping to the higher accountancy, various commercial laws and hence I could obtain proficiency in banking. After working at various offices for about 15 years we teamed again at Zonal Staff Training Center as faculty. There again he helped me a lot to develop myself as an expert faculty. The other friend Shri Madhusudan Tarkas who has mastery over English, also was instrumental in my career as a professional banker. He is a person with a magnanimous heart. He had a wonderful memory and could recollect the folio numbers of the client even after a year. I am fortunate that our trio has a close relationship even more than earlier days.

I loved to be amongst the people right from my school days. I was known to everybody in the colony and had an easy access in all the 110 houses. This had helped me in my Banking career a lot. In branches I always used to move in various departments and amongst the customers, knowing what was going on. This customer and staff connect had an immense effect on mobilization of business and effective management. In fact this was the Managerial theory propounded by Tom Peters known as 'Management by Walk Around'. I always followed an open door policy thereby I was a very approachable and available person to one and all. I got an opportunity to work in over 30 different offices / branches in three different States. I could easily make good friendship with very poor customers as well very affluent Billionaire customers because I am having an affinity towards human beings. This had helped me to easily win over several customers for the bank. I may quote an indelible incident; on my retirement day one of the liftmen requested me to hand over my Mobile phone for half an hour and while returning it, told that he had recorded 50 odd Marathi old songs in the memory chip. Sir, 'This is a small gift from me at your retirement.' I was overwhelmed by his gesture and I swore it was the most **Cherishable gift** of my life.

Whatever success I could achieve during my 40+ years of banking career, was the result of reliable staff, customers and a bridge of faith built between us. The other reason was that throughout my career my style of Leadership was Democratic except maybe at one or two emergent occasions.

I was motivated to write this book so that the managers working in financial institutions will find a guide to refer and arrive at a solution while confronting the difficult situations.

In this book I have shared more than 51 different episodes; those had an impact on my Banking life. The book is sub divided into nine chapters and in each chapter there are stories/episodes depicting various situations where managerial skills, techniques, and leadership qualities were tested extensively. The chapter No. 3 containing 'Mentors in my Banking Career' gives an insight into the art of mentoring the people who are working with you. This is explained by quoting the example of Ex CMD of Syndicate Bank and Bank of India, late Mr. K. V. Krishnamurty, who was the then Branch Head where the author was working. The tips embodied in the chapter no. 3 on 'Administration' will be an excellent guide to the persons working in HR department. It explains by quoting the live examples of negotiating skills, reconciliation and method of tactfully handling difficult situations. The heart of banking, 'The Customer Service' elaborated in chapter number 4, how the author could get 'The Wow from the customers' by slightly tweaking rules and regulations, creating faith and confidence in the minds of the customers and winning them over for the institution. The Human angle of the banker is reflected through various experiences in the stories such as 'Free Lance

Marketing Officer, 'How Are You Concerned?' and others. The author has shown by his own experience that while social responsibilities are fulfilled, simultaneously the Institutional well being can also be taken care of. Reading chapter no. 6 'The difficult situations faced' gives an insight how an important thing not attended on time translates into an urgent one. It teaches how to get over the difficult situation by tactfully handling it while keeping oneself absolutely cool. The inference drawn from the chapter is that, in difficult situations you are always alone and have to wade through and find your own path with grit. The episode, 'Operation, 81 Cheques' is a real stunner, in the sense how so many instruments go mysteriously missing and how such a difficult situation was handled with a cool mind. The skill, the grit, the empathy towards the staff, the team work, planning, execution and the perseverance required for obtaining the duplicates of all those missing cheques and that too without any complaint from the customers, is exemplary. Similarly, transforming the rustic old branch into a branch with all modern facilities having a look of a Heritage Branch with the help of the General Administration Department of Central Office was a daunting task, full of hurdles right from convincing the staff, staff unions and that too without a day's discontinuity in work as there were 125 work stations to be shifted to and fro from one building to the other. The task was handled deftly with a professional touch without disturbing the Customer Service. It is a success story how one should work in a team by application of all management skills right from motivation to preparation of a plan, delegation, communication, time management and what not? Reading the book one will understand how all Managerial responsibilities can be fulfilled keeping the thread of human relations at its heart/ central place and weaving the net work of the customers for the ultimate benefit of the Institution. I trust it will be an insightful and inspiring handy book to the Managers working not only in the Banks but also in other financial services and other service industries where human relationship is involved. Similarly the students of management will find it extremely helpful to basically understand the principles of management propounded in various management theories and their practical applications.

I am sure that a common reader will find these stories interesting because of the flow of narration, lucid language and the social dimension as entwined by a practical banker.

Thus this book contains both 'The knowledge acquired' and 'The knowledge experienced' which would be of immense help to the reader.

Waman Gokhale

Acknowledgements

I have been inspired and helped by many colleagues for writing my experiences in the form of a book. I acknowledge the major contributors to my endeavour. While writing this book Mr. Tarkas my old pal was a great help suggesting the cast of the book, dimensions to be included and appropriate words to suit the different situations. Sitting at Akola, a far off place from Pune, we were in constant touch through the mobile even at odd hours. I am thankful for the silent contribution from his wife Mrs. Nandabhabi. I am equally grateful to English professors Mrs. Shubhangi and Mr.Nitin Jarindikar from Kohlapur, who had very painstakingly corrected the manuscript, suggested the modifications to be carried out so that the book will have a real value addition in the practical field of management. I got valuable suggestions and encouragement from Mr. Ashok Kumar from my parent bank for which I am thankful. I would be remiss in my debt in my not acknowledgement to my family members Smita, Snehal, Sameer, Shridhar and Surbhi. Lastly, I express my thanks to Shri Dattatraya Pashte of Dimond Publications and their staff particularly to artist Mr. Shamkant Bhalekar who had transformed my ideas into a wonderful book.

Waman Gokhale

Table of Contents

Chapter – 5 : Social Engineering

Chapter – 6 : Difficult Situations Faced during Banking Career

Chapter – 7 : Facing Angry Customers

Chapter – 8 Applying Managerial Skills and Techniques

1 | LESSONS IN BANKING

(1) Hall-Mark of a Banker

It was the month of April 1975, a very busy season for the Tendu leaf merchants (Leaves for manufacturing Beedies) and hence for our branch also. The leaves were sold by auction by the forest department and the merchants would buy through the auction and then sell ultimately to the manufacturer of Beedies. One of the conditions for application for the auction was that the tender should be accompanied with a Fixed Deposit of 10 % of the value of the tender. Our branch was located in a strategic place thick with such Traders and was a leading Bank in the city. On some busy days we used to get 60 to100 applications for issuance of deposits in favour of 'The DFO A B C, Division, ..., Account X Y Z.' The amount of deposit would decide the **competitive tender amount** filled in by the merchant. In fact every merchant was interested to understand what amount of fixed deposit had been prepared by others in the competitive bid.

I was busy on one of the days in April, accepting the applications for deposit and then issuing the deposit receipts after completing all the requisite formalities. Then Mr. Navinbhai, who was one of the best customers of the branch, approached me. He wanted to understand from me the deposit amount received from our other client Mr. Dineshbhai, his competitor. I smiled at him and in a very polite but straightway refused to share the information with him. He got a bit irritated and said, I could oversee all the deposit receipts sitting across you. I again smiled at him and asked him 'Sir, please let me know if Mr. Dineshbhai or any other person makes a similar request about the deposit amounts received from you, what would be your expectations? 'He received the answer and shown his concurrence.'

Then I said further, 'So far as your overseeing was concerned, the information was not reveled by me and that was my duty. Sir, for you it was exactly the similar case of founder of a lost article and you too as a gentleman had a duty'!

After a fortnight or so, our Branch Manager called me and informed that a high value tender had been won by Mr. Naveenbhai. He had narrated the whole episode to our Branch Manager and appreciated me for maintaining a tradition of trust and faith for which our Bank was known.

Our Branch Manager also very affectionately patted me!

Take Away :

➢ **Banking is nothing but creating a faith and confidence in the minds of the customers.**

➢ **Always maintain a high standard of secrecy while dealing with customers and imbibe a habit to say 'No', with a smile and in a very polite way.**

• • •

(2) My Second Lesson in Banking

It was the 1'st day of the month and I was occupying the Foreign Exchange Counter facing the big entrance gate of Nagpur Main branch along with my officer colleague Mr. Pereira. It was a big branch with around 100 plus staff. Almost all work was handled manually.

As soon as the front door was opened at 10.30 am, we received 5 to 6 pensioners who were unable to fill in withdrawal slips and approached Mr. Pereira occupying the table, which was right in front of the gate. He helped them. Two foreigners were also ready for encashing their foreign currency traveller's cheques.

They were welcomed with a smile. He obtained the passport and very politely enquired about the place where they belong to as well the cities they visited in India. At the same time he was completing the formalities and simultaneously explaining to me the procedure to be followed, the vouching to be done, the intricacy of Card rates and of the various Buying and Selling rates. He then moved to the cash department and brought the cash to be handed over to the foreign tourists. Of course before hand he had sought from them the denominations of the currency notes they would prefer. There was a telephone call from someone requesting whether her Fixed Deposits were ready and should she visit during the afternoon to collect the same. On obtaining the information from the concerned department confirmation was conveyed back to her in a very pleasing tone.

Another customer was ready with documents as he wanted a Bank Guarantee to be issued urgently which was to be deposited in lieu of the tender money. It was necessary to prepare the process note to be put up before the Branch Manager for sanction. On receiving sanction, type out the guarantee, counter guarantee, seek the deposit, recover the commission and complete rest of the requisite formalities. In those days there were only typewriters and no computers. He called on the typist Mrs. Julie, enquired about the health of her ailing mother and then discussed how to go ahead with the BG. She with a smile responded, assuring to ready the guarantee, counter guarantee and also a forwarding letter too within no time.

Thus very deftly he was handling various jobs as well giving lessons to me not only in the procedural drudgery but also the practices in human relationship. He was called by the Branch Manager for some query in respect of the matter related with mortgage of another branch office. A saving deposit customer in the mean time sought his help as he could not get the Cheque Book from the concerned counter, this was also attended too.

We were performing our daily chores when two blind customers came up for depositing money in their Saving Bank account. They were given counter service there and there, he did not forget to get their pass books updated and communicated them the available balance in the account.

We then broke for lunch recess. One of the staff members accompanying another colleague appeared after the lunch time. He desired help from Mr. Pereira to get admission for his son in one of the schools. Mr. Pereira did speak with the concerned school authorities and arranged for admission. Mr.Gururaj an officer colleague wanted his help to check the ledgers at the end of the day as he had to go early to take his wife to a doctor. And a hearty smile was his response.

At the end of the day, we departed with our accountant and Branch Manager. Of course I was amazed by his daily routine and asked him where from he derives such an enormous energy? He enlightened me 'I am a devout Christan. I do not have much time to serve the society and hence I attend to one and all the persons so as to fulfill my social obligations.'

Now, after looking back towards my 40 plus years of service, I feel myself extremely fortunate to meet such a wonderful human being that too at the beginning of my banking career who had an immense impact on my making. I could copy some of his virtues and hence always had an ease as well as happiness of working with people. He taught me multi tasking, team work, interpersonal relationship, how to smile while working, kindness, importance of service to the human being and what not. My banking experience was enriched by him and thereby I had a very cordial relationship with my customers throughout my service rather I would say it became a part of my DNA.

Take Away :

> **A good customer service agent is one who has the right mix of <u>head and a heart</u>. One who <u>enjoys</u> his work and has the <u>right attitude</u> towards life. Of all the qualities <u>ATTITUDE</u> is the most important one.**

• • •

(3) Envelope Number 1367

All of us were searching an envelope for about an hour, but could not lay hands on it. The bunch of Dak had moved from my table to the desk of Mr. Shah, our supervisor and then to our Daftari and back. But except the envelope number 1367 all other 78 registered envelopes from 1301 to 1378 were intact.

It was the beginning of my career as a banker. I was handling the despatch department. The despatch department used to be a life line in those days as all the work in the banks were handled manually. The branches and the controlling offices were connected either through post (Dak), telegrams or telephones. The branches used to send various advices called as MF (Manifold) to each other through which most of the accounting entries between the branches and controlling offices used to take place. The remittances were commonly sent through Demand Drafts. The goods were exchanged between the buyers and sellers living in different cities mostly through the banks. Hence bills accompanied with RRs, MTRs or LRs and Trade Invoices were sent to the Banks and against these the funds used to be remitted through a MF or a DD. Even in medium sized branches the despatch used to be a busy department. In such branches it was usual that daily there would be Registered Dak consisting of 75 to100 envelopes. As per the prevailed system all the addresses on the envelopes were hand written and then entries were recorded in a despatch register and again in the Register provided by Postal Department for registered Dak. It would then be sent to the supervisor for checking; on return to the despatcher it would be handed over to the Daftari for inserting the documents, pasting the label with registered number on the envelope and then closing the envelopes to be carried to the post office. However on that day, it was observed by Daftari that the envelope no 1367 was not traceable. All of us were scared as the concerned envelope contained the document of very high value.

We searched the drawers, the boxes, the trays, waste paper baskets and what not. All of us were non plussed and perplexed. Looking all of us worried, our Head Peon Shri Pande aged about sixty, who was hardly literate to say as he could write his name, came near and said, "Kya hum dekhe?" (May I look?). Nobody answered, but on his own he took all the envelopes in hand and with a scissor started opening each envelope very carefully. We all were looking at him with distrust. However he was attaining the job very meticulously. He had reached almost at the last Registry numbering 1377, and Oh! Gosh! It really happened that the missing Envelope 1367 was inserted in that last but one envelope. Now Shri Pandeji was smiling at all of us beneath his voluminous moustache and said, **'Humre bal aise hi safed nahi whoea!' (My wisdom is through experience).**

All of us silently saluted him.

Take Away :

> **If Intelligence is Gold, experience is Platinum.**

● ● ●

(4) Manifold Mystery

I was working in one of the branches at Nagpur I was handling the Cash Book, General Ledger, Balance Book, Central Office Accounts department. One morning I was called by Mr. Ahemed, Accountant of our Branch and he instructed me to prepare and send a duplicate statement of a particular day in respect of Central Office (CO) Account, an account through which settlement of inter branch transactions takes place. He informed me that there was a letter from CO, that they had not received the statement of that particular day. I called our Daftari Shri Ravi who was assigned the work of safe keeping of the records, to bring the bound duplicate copy of the concerned statement. However for the duplicate I also called for the vouchers of Central Office account for the concerned day, as taught to us by our superiors that whenever a duplicate of any such nominal account was to be prepared refer original. After repeatedly calling Shri Ravi for the vouchers, he did not bring them. He, afterwards, told me that he was unable to lay hands on the relevant vouchers. He further commented that perhaps the lot of voucher was wrongly filed with the vouchers of some other day. I informed this to Mr. Ahmed. Simultaneously I called for the Despatch Register and on verifying found that the CO statements of the relevant date as well as other three days were properly despatched as per entry in the register. This fact was also brought to the knowledge of the accountant. I vividly remember that despite these shortcomings our Accountant insisted me to prepare a duplicate CO statement based on the available records. As per his instructions the Duplicate was prepared by me; however I did record the fact in the register that CO statement was based on records and in absence of the relevant original vouchers. I also insisted Mr. Ahmed to put his signature as confirmation of his orders. This was done by me purely because of some inner instinct.

After about three weeks we received a stringent reminder from CO that despite their earlier instructions they had not received the CO statement of the day. The reminder was directed to me, I again verified the despatch register of the day of our preparing the duplicate for second time. The entry was very much there in the register. I again tried to find out the vouchers of the day but failed. Now I smelt something foul and approached another officer since Mr. Ahmed was on leave. We together verified all the records of the day and were shocked that several vouchers pertaining to the day and credited to a particular account were missing. On in-depth verification it came out that some culprit utilizing the parent branch manifold and Mail Transfer Vouchers had fraudulently raised the entries through the CO account and credited to a fictitious Savings Account. The amount credited was about Rs20,000/-. It was a substantial sum at that time if you compare the monthly salary of Rs. 800/-received at that time by me. The entire amount had already been withdrawn.

It was clear that a fraud was perpetuated. We reported the details to our Regional Office. In due course an Auditor was deputed for a detailed inquiry. On one strange day I received a memorandum from RO seeking the explanation and I literally went into frenzy, as I was the one who detected the fraud. Even one of my colleagues also received a Memo as he had opened the account. Here also I very vividly remember that I had refused to open that account as I had some odd feelings. But then the cause of my refusal was, I was working on the counter for sometime in absence of the usual Clark.

We were under a tremendous pressure, but leaders of our Union assured us that they would fight it out as there was no question of our involvement. We furnished the explanation to the memo to our higher authorities and it was accepted, but we did suffer an agony for about a month.

Take Away :

- ➢ **Always create a written record of all the odd or unusual things which you may observe.**
- ➢ **An intuition is a great friend, always learn to pick up the signal and act on it.**

2 | MENTORS IN MY BANKING CAREER

(1) Colleagues at Gondia

We had a fantastic team of generation Y when I joined Gondia (Maharashtra) branch in 1973. I was the junior most in the branch, a direct recruit straight from The Institute of Science, not knowing even A B C of banking. My friend and the first mentor in my Banking career was of course Shri Hemant Wankhede, a Gold Medalist and Post Graduate student of Commerce. He had an uncanny art of teaching. He taught me right from fundamentals of double entry book keeping to the higher accountancy; as well various commercial laws in a very lucid language. He motivated the entire Y brigade to join Indian Institute of Banking for membership. He also created a competitive spirit amongst us to gain the Certified Associated status of Indian Institute of Banker's referred as CAIIB. I could become a certified associate of I.I.B. because of his pursuance and as a result I could obtain proficiency in banking. After working at various other offices for about 15 years we teamed again at Zonal Staff Training Center, Pune as a faculty member. There also he was my mentor and helped me a lot to develop me as a skilled faculty. The other friend was Shri Madhusudan Tarkas who has a mastery over English. He is a person with a magnanimous heart. He has a wonderful memory and could recollect the folio numbers of the client even after passage of years. He was a perfectionist. Another colleague Mr. Chako Kuriakose was M.A. with English literature. He was bestowed with two of the most sought after skills of life, one effective communication and the other possessing heart of a child. He used to say, 'Concise messages are more appealing and comprehensible to the audience' and would always redraft our letters so that we could understand and emulate his knack. He was very naughty and would cut fancy jokes. I am tempted to give an example.

He had twin daughters. On visit to his residence, one of our colleagues asked him, 'Who is Jenny and who is Julie?' He immediately came out, 'I am also always confused!'

He was the senior most amongst us and that his wages were double than what I was drawing. Once while sitting across and working on some returns, the tip of my pencil was broken. Instantly he handed over his pencil saying, 'Bank should not lose because of time waste and he sat watching me!'

He once told, 'Today Mr. Pole, an officer with some whips of white hair in his stylish beard visited us, Jennie looking at his beard retorted, 'Papa-Papa, look! Uncle has come to us brushing the teeth!'

Once we were very busy with closing work, perhaps it was my first experience of the closing year in my banking career. I was not so clear about two aspects and so innocently asked Mr. Chako, 'Some information formats are called as 'Statements' and others are Returns', how is it?' The answer was instantaneous, 'When a Statement is submitted to RO/ZO/CO/HO and returned back for correction and then resubmitted it is called as Return!'

I cherish his memory but did not have contact for over30 years. Because of his presence the work life used to be very lively!

He taught me these two skills of life which proved to be very handy to become a successful banker!

Initially I was helped a lot by the sub staff working as my colleague right from entries in various books of accounts, ledgers, registers, the work flow and what not. I learnt the art of filing papers, documents of various sizes in a File in such a way that a single paper would not come out and all papers will be in such a symmetry from all the three sides as if cut by a razor sharp knife. I am thankful to Shri Arjun, the then Daftari at our office for making me an expert in this skill.

Take Away :

❯ **Some simple skills can make your work life happy.**

❯ **The knowledge comes to us from all Universe!**

● ● ●

(2) My Branch Managers/Heads

Branch Heads played an important role in my making. I duplicated/cloned several virtues from them like handling the staff, leadership qualities, time management and what not. I had a nostalgic memory of all these stalwarts.

❖ **Late Shri S.T.Sapre** was my first Branch Manager; he was a short statured person like me and used to be dressed very elegantly. He was also a smart worker. In the morning if he was entering the cabin, it must be **10.00 am**, we would say 'Ghadi Aa Gayi!' (That means a watch has arrived). He was very punctual in his appointments with customers. He used to have very close information not only of the staff members but also the near and dear relatives of the staff. He would enquire with say Mr.Naik, 'How is your father? How about his sugar level?' Or with Mr. Shah, 'Whether your elder son now settled in hostel?' He would enquire with sub staff Shri Pandeji, 'How about repairing of your house?' He would be equally at ease with the customers while enquiring about their lives. He used to visit every counter in the branch and with a Hawk's eye would see to it that the systems and procedures are followed without any short cuts by us and would correct us where necessary.

❖ **Late Shri Malge** was a fatherly figure. He was a simple down to earth person. If some staff member fell ill and approached him for permission to leave early, he would ask, 'Shall I make arrangement to drop you home and ask my wife to send Tiffin with Khichadi to you?' He would suggest some medicine or even provide a tablet from his bag. I vividly remember one Closing Year when unions had called a Work to Rule agitation Programme, Non cooperation with management etc. He single handedly completed applying interest in all the Savings bank accounts numbering over 3500 and distributed in 12 different ledgers. This had an indelible effect on us and then all of us completed the allotted closing work for 'Shri Malge sahib' in spite of Work to Rule call from the union. For this single reason Shri Malge sahib along with the humanitarian approach has remained in my memory.

❖ **Late Shri Deshpande** lovingly referred as 'AS' because of his initials. He was a 'persona special for me.' He was gifted with several skills. He was a friend of everybody and had an ability to read a person with his single sharp gaze, perhaps with intuition. While processing the loan proposals, particularly at the time of Interviewing he would ask such questions to the borrower or guarantor which would not be intimidating but he would get the feedback necessary to understand and decide about the proposal. For an example, he would ask a guarantor in his calm and composed voice, 'Now a days we frequently stood as guarantor to our friends or relatives even I had given such guarantee, please let me know about you so as to just fill in point no 12 in our format to complete the formalities.' Such questions mostly elicit the correct information. This is one of the most vital information but difficult to answer and is wrongly reported as NIL. The things have not changed even today.

You would always find him mixing with business community, visiting their homes, shops, galas, even at pan shops, marriages and socializing with them. These were the places to understand the health of the borrower; yes I am talking about financial health and the standing of the borrowers which were and are the time tested fundamentals while arriving at a Credit Decision and what we call now 'Know Your Customer' compliance. Remember I am talking of 1976 when focus of appraisal was worth of the borrower which has now shifted to the viability of the enterprise.

- Mr.Deshpande was equally comfortable while handling the staff matters. I would cite two examples:

During the closing period while distributing the work he would call a staff meeting and let everyone pickup the part, for any remaining part of the work he will straight away assign it to senior staff. Similarly the Duty list which was and still is a bone of contention in the branches was handled by him in a similar democratic style. Of course he will always hold one or two departments like Advances, Fixed Deposits etc. with him to be assigned to a selected staff. I acquired these two key skills from him. He was a Branch Manager, always appreciating the good performance of the staff.

I still feel that he will come some day and pat me when something good is performed.

> **Mr. R. K. Joshi**

He was a famous person known to every second man in Amravati and I had an opportunity to work with him. He would help out to anybody and everybody without discrimination, if little air is blown. Higher authorities and even the staff working at administrative offices would always address him as a Leader of the District and would get almost everything done through him. His public contacts were phenomenal and he could get the things moving even from thick skinned Government officials. His contribution in respect of opening of over 30 branches in a single District was really praiseworthy. On 14th Nov1981, 6 branches were opened on a single day. He had excellent marketing skills and did make use of it in multiplying the business for the bank. He was also instrumental in making available affordable houses to all staff members in the district by extending the Housing Loans, even by going out of way if necessary. I am personally thankful to him as I was also a benefactor. None of those accounts had any problems. By heart he was a very kind and helpful person but this was one of the reasons of his downfall. Although in respect of some loan accounts he faced problems but he was a lion hearted person and took the entire blame and responsibility on himself. At no moment of time he had shown a finger towards any other staff. My hats off to his courage and sportive spirit to accept the blame playfully.

❖ **Mr.KVK** – Yes, you are right he was late **Mr. K V Krishnamurthy who was my Branch Manager at Nagpur M.O., who later on became our Regional Manager and subsequently CMD of Syndicate Bank and Bank of India.** He was a Chartered Accountant and the first real professional banker with whom I had an opportunity to work. He was a very persuasive and tough personality to deal with. He was very quick in decision making and always used to rely on his trusted handpicked staff, of course the concerned staff member had to undergo a close scrutiny. I remember, when a BG proposal or for that matter any proposal was put up for consideration he would ask 4 to 5 questions and would decide the fate thereof at hand. The key perhaps was the experience he gained while working as an internal auditor of the bank for over 3years, the professional acumen and of course the intellect which he had in ample. He used to recognize talent and would be dismissing the unwanted people if at all they come around. He would take you around for inspection of the Industry as well as branch offices and elicit the information required for making the inspection fruitful. Generally he would ask the questions which would yield the necessary information or he would randomly pick up books of accounts, say Sundry Creditors or Debtors account ledger and cross check the earlier answers given to him in respect of the Credit period enjoyed or given (to the customers) to understand the truthfulness. Likewise at the time of branch inspection searching questions would be put up on vital parameters like per head business etc., so that the BM had to remain always prepared. In his regime all the officers too had to be always on the toes as he would pick up the telephone at any time and get directly connected for the first hand information.

All these vital managerial aspects came very handy to me while working not only as a Branch Manager but also as a Regional Manager and as a Chief Internal Auditor, Mumbai.

His way of dealing was straight forward and no hanky panky business. He had a very tacit way of tackling the Union Leaders. I would quote one such wordy tussle:

It was around 11 am. We were in the cabin discussing some L C issue when a Union Leader in his usual style entered and directly sat across Mr.KVK. When KVK saw some bandage on the left hand of the leader, he asked with a wry smile, 'What? Who?' Leader replied, 'I did not know that you were out. I visited your house yesterday. Your dog is really ferocious. He pounced upon me and bit me.' Mr.KVK quipped, **'That day I was telling our Zonal Manager, not only me but even my dog can sniff the Union Leaders, <u>now he will agree.</u>'**

Take Away

➢ **Connect with staff and customers**

➢ **Imbibe in you the spirit of discipline and punctuality.**

➢ **People around you recognize the value of personal caring.**

➢ **Body language and personal touch like patting are parts of most effective communications.**

➢ **Too much energy and dynamism is fatal.**

➢ **Always build a Net Work of people from all areas.**

➢ **One must learn the art of saying 'No.'**

➢ **The situation decides which the best leadership style is.**

➢ **On one hand control the staff and leave the other leash a bit loose to give space to the staff for self development. It is the hallmark of a true leader.**

➤ Develop the art to open your third eye i.e. intuition while arriving at crucial decisions.

The concept of Leadership Shadowing

Imagine if you get to be by the CEO's side for few days, how much you would learn? How much exposure you would get? How inspired you would be by his/her unique methods of dealing with problems? How motivated would you be to aim to be? If you knew how exactly his/her work day unfolded?

The shadowing of the leaders helps the participant learn from observing the leader and ready to excel in future leadership roles by developing the key requisites / skills. It is said that 70% of learning comes from on the job; leadership shadowing is the key to foster talent.

It also ensures that the leaders take time to invest in nurturing future talent. The advantages :

1) Enables the participant a top-down approach to leadership and appreciate business strategy.
2) Enables participants to learn the art of net-working influencing and develop executive presence early in the career.
3) Enables participants to get mentored by seasoned head.
4) Provides participants an opportunity to experiment early, take responsibility and develop maturity.
5) Enables participant to go up a steep learning curve on business and capabilities/behaviours.

• • •

(3) Mentors at Training Center

My tenure at ZSTC at Pune was one of the memorable parts of my banking life. This was a place where I developed various life skills in the august presence and mentorship of our Faculty Leader Mr. Nagnoor. He was not only a fatherly figure but had several qualities and skills. His writing skills were really praise worthy. He had an ability to write pages after pages without a single mistake. He was so versatile that one could get guidance on any subject say, how to cook a particular dish to the International norms on Lending to infrastructure. He could easily engage classes for entire day without break and jokingly used to say, 'Watch the calendar and not a clock.' He had an ability to engage classes' right from sub staff to very senior staff on any subject. For all of us he was an encyclopedia and whenever we used to stuck up on any subject, he was a ready reckoner. He had given us full liberty to study, work and develop various subjects and thus played an important role in my making.

I had all praise for my other colleagues Mr. Mujumder, Mr. Choudhary and my brotherly mate Shri Hemant who helped me not only to stand and deliver the subjects effectively but also the intricacies of class control. During the Trainer's Training Programme we had a wonderful master trainer Mr. Suterwala who shared all the skills required for a faculty. He taught how to stand, how to use hands, the posture, the gestures, the gaze, voice control etc. He also explained how to prepare a lesson plan and PPT's. While describing the importance of first few words in any presentation, he used to say, 'Blow your trumpet loudly.' His presentations used to be very lively and action packed. He would also show the things to be avoided. I salute him for sharing all his tricks of the trade which helped me to be a successful faculty. Similarly the teachers who had an immense effect on my communication skills definitely were the Trainees I met and would meet.

The first important workshop was conducted at Nagpur R.O. It was my first outing and the programme was for the veteran Branch Managers, many of them were our bosses during the past. The workshop was to refresh the knowledge on Credit Management and was immediately on the beginning of opening of our Economy in 1998. We have to first break the ice, i.e. remove the prejudice from the minds of the seniors that, what these youngsters would teach them? And then to create a level playing field for us. We began with a tough Pre Training exercise based on the latest changes that would be soon a part of the financial system. Seniors were hardly able to solve the questions and there was a vociferous request that the marks scored should not be announced. Thus we won the first bout. Then during our first session we began by recognizing our Ex. Branch Managers and acknowledging that our first baby steps in the area of Financing were with the help of those seniors. These words had such an impact that the group accepted us as faculty. I need not say that, then it was a cakewalk for us and the workshop was a total success.

Take Away :

- ➤ **For a big and important event strategic planning is the key.**
- ➤ **Always recognize and acknowledge the people you know while delivering a lecture. This immensely improves your acceptability.**
- ➤ **One learns a lot while teaching.**
- ➤ **When we teach, we gain new insight, we learn at a deeper level and our learning expands.**

3 | HUMAN RELATIONS

(1) Handling Administration

It took long time to establish myself as the Chief Manager, in charge of Central Staff Department (CSD) an Administration wing at CO Mumbai with about 1200 staff. The department comprise of two wings, one looking after the Salary, Income Tax and the other about the Placement of all the staff members from Sub Staff level to Senior Manager (Scale III) and the disciplinary action; TA bills, LFC bills, Medical bills, Leave and attendance, Terminal Benefits, Loans etc. The department was looking after these benefits in respect of all the person's working in CO, right from Chairman and Managing Director to the lowest Cadre i.e. a part time sweeper. In addition to this conducting various Recruitment Tests was also the part of my duties.

One of the toughest tasks was placement on promotion and rotation of staff as it involved interest of all the 4 to 5 unions, welfare organizations, individual staff and the Executives like GM's, DGM's, etc. All the Unions of the Award Staff were very strong and their strength was more or less equal. Whereas most of the officer staff belonged to one union. The leaders and their unions were quite militant and could easily create pressure because of their sheer strength. The problems were multi faceted, as Staff residing in South Mumbai always wanted their postings in that area; whereas staff residing on Central railway, Harbour line and Western line always demanded posting at the offices located on those lines.

It simply means that if you satisfy one, at least three other entities would be there against you. I remember having faced one such agitation against me immediately after joining at CSD. At least fifty to sixty staff members stormed in my cabin, raising their usual slogans and they continued like that for some time. Then their leader in a very high pitch told me how I had violated some norms and how injustice was done. I could not understand properly what they wanted and I was sure they too had no real objectives. I very quietly heard all that had been said and told that I would look into the matter. After shouting slogans for about half an hour they dispersed. On their departure my immediate second-in-command came in and told Sir, 'You had been successful in facing the trial by the union.' They appreciated you that you stood and faced them calmly as well listened to them, this is their way to provocate and test. This was the first lesson I learnt in the art of negotiation. The other Union Leader with some of his members also called on me and told me that I should not favour anybody and succumb to pressure. It was just like a walk on a tightly tied rope to balance all the stake holders. But if you face the challenges you had the fruits of it in the form of self confidence and satisfaction.

During 3 years of working at CSD, I had many such occasions where I had to face many critical situations. However my decisions were always for the ultimate benefit of the staff. During my tenure I had seen that my department do act as a Service Provider and it was always our endeavour to find out the solutions to the problems rather than precipitating them. I remember several Staff housing loan cases sanctioned in a day's time even by going out of frame work. Several staff members coming from outside States used to approach for introductory letters for admission in the Reputed Hospitals for their kith and kin for critical operations without depositing cash and were always helped. I did help through our Branch Managers of Tata Memorial Cancer Hospital for admission and treatment of staff or their relatives suffering from cancer. I did all these activities as if they were a part of my duty.

Take Away :

➤ While negotiating always observe that it will be a win-win situation for both the sides.

➤ First understand the views of the others and then only expect that others will understand you.

➤ Always take all the people together with you (i.e. Synergize).

• • •

(2) Reconciliation

One day I was sitting alone in my cabin. At around 4pm a middle aged lady staff Mrs. Vrunda, slightly known came to me. She requested me to spare sometime as she wanted some help for one of her colleagues. On my assent she narrated her story. In their department one gentleman named Mr. Sundeep was working for last 3to4 years. He was a very regular and a knowledgeable employee of the Forex Department. But for last 6 months, he was very irregular in attendance, had no concentration in work and making silly mistakes. He remained absent without any application. His immediate boss had approached me for transferring him. She further told me that there was some problem on his home front since she was observing change in his behaviour for last several months. She said the boy was really good and needs help. She requested me to do something. Sir, 'I feel you are the only right person known to me who can bring some positive change in him.' I asked with her about the place where he resides and any other staff known to her, who resides in the same locality. She told me the names of two staff members living near Mr. Sundeep and known to her. I was not sure how to proceed. However I called my deputy who was in the department for about 4years and known to be a very reasonable person. I requested him to let me know the staff living near Mr. Sundeep. He enquired, Sir 'Are you referring to the staff from Forex Department.?' On my saying 'Yes', he gave me 5to6 contacts. Out of those, he suggested me about one officer Mr. Roy. He told Mr. Roy to meet me the next day at around 2pm. We met on Saturday, I briefed Mr. Roy about Mr. Sundeep. He told me that he too belonged to the home town of Mr. Sundeep. He knew Mr. Sundeep's wife. They were acquainted with each other as once they had met at a religious place. I requested Mr. Roy to visit their home casually and since he too was fluent with Bangala, try to find out what was the problem and inform me in a day or two.

Mr. Roy briefed me as follows; Mrs. Savita, Sundeep's wife, belonged to a rich family. They had a very huge house at her native place and her father was a senior Government official. Whereas here in Mumbai they had a very small one bed room flat in a congested locality. Mr. Sundeep used to leave the house at 7.30 am and would return home at about 8 pm. She was all alone in the home having no social contacts. Further Sundeep was in the clerical cadre. She was like a fish out of water. Having all this information I called Mr. Sundeep and his departmental colleague Mrs. Vrunda. He initially thought I had called him for some departmental action for his absence. But his colleague Mrs. Vrunda really did well the important job of ice breaking and Sundeep opened up. He informed me that his wife feels alone and repeatedly compares her family with his. She makes hue and cry at the time of leaving for office and hence he was not his usual self, as such he was very irregular. He then requested me to speak with his wife. Sir, 'She may listen to you.'

On the next Saturday, we decided to meet at about 2 pm i.e. after office hours. I deliberately called Mr. Roy so that while speaking with Mrs. Savita language would not be a barrier. On the decided day, we all met. Mr. Roy began in Bangla and perhaps he spoke some good things about her parents. He told that I was a highly placed authority and very helping to the staff. He made the environment very congenial and then I spoke. I told her that soon I would be transferring Mr. Sundeep to a nearby branch from the residence. I assured her that Mr. Sundeep was eligible for promotion. He was a brilliant boy and definitely would be successful and soon be an officer. He may be placed at any suitable place in India. If she helped Mr. Sundeep, this would happen and

I appealed her to take his care. So far as his preparation for examination is concerned, I would guide him but then he has to be in CO and spare some time. Mr. Roy at that instant told her that he would tell his wife and acquaint her with two /three Bengali families. She understood it well and agreed. Our meeting ended on a positive note. There onwards Mr. Sundeep was regular in attendance. As promised, I did help him to prepare for the examination. He scored well. In due course the family grew to four members and presently Mr. Sundeep is in Scale II in some branch in West Bengal.

Take Away :

➤ **An administrator should master the art of reconciliation.**
➤ **He should be able to step into the shoes of the other person.**

● ● ●

(3) 26/7 Mumbai Deluge :

For last few days, it was raining heavily during Monsoon. It was Monday and as usual I caught a bus at 5.30 am from Pune for Mumbai. There was hardly any traffic on the Express Highway, particularly from Mumbai towards Pune. We had to stop at two places because of the land slides. However our bus could reach Nariman Point Mumbai at around 10 am sheerly because our driver had a good knowledge of roads in Mumbai. We had to cross several inundated roads near Parel, Lalbaugh areas. I directly got in my office. There were very thick clouds hanging in the sky and moving speedily as winds were blowing at high speed. The sea was very rough and there were clear cut indications of a storm. Only some buses were plying and that too very slowly because of the water logging. The Suburban trains, being the life line of Mumbai were also plying at a snail's pace as in low lying areas water was flowing over the rail tracks. We allowed the late coming and some staff literally reported at around 11.30 am instead of 10 am. On TV and radio channels, there was a warning of heavy to extremely heavy rains, but it was treated as a part of Mumbai Monsoon. The traffic stood at a standstill at around 12.30 pm. There were announcements on railway stations that trains were stuck up and will be late for indefinite time. The staff had broken for lunch at about 1.30 pm and they started requesting to allow them to go home. It was difficult but in consultation with DGM (HRD), they were allowed as a special case.

It was announced that three to four areas in Mumbai and around there were cloud bursts and hence there were extremely heavy rains. Most of the roads were looking as if they were the canals made for water supplies. All the traffic air, rail and road came to a grinding halt. Although we had warned the staff particularly to the ladies, not to venture out, they still went to the VT (CST), Churchgate railway stations to reach home. The journey usually costs about Rs. 8 to 10, but very few Taxis were plying and exorbitantly charged up-to Rs 100. All these staff members ultimately returned from station to Central Office (CO) by 7 pm, walking in heavy rains as there was no place even on railway stations to stand. The condition, particularly of ladies staff was precarious as some body's husband, daughter, son etc. were caught and stranded at their offices, schools, railway stations, bus stations or other places as everywhere there was water. Some people ventured out, and had to walk 8 to 10 Kms. in the dirty water and ultimately reached their homes at about 11pm to 5 am next day. They suffered a lot having travelled in the dirty water. Some staff members had their houses fully inundated in water and their house hold goods were literally taken away by flowing water. Mobile phones, land lines and electricity links were also broken and hence there was total communication failure. At CO there were at least 350 staff out of 650 and ladies staff was about 100. Fortunately in the area there was no failure of electricity. It was already 8 pm and all the nearby hotels, road side eateries were closed down. We had a canteen at CO but as usual the cooks had left the canteen at about 12.30 pm Now we had only serving staff at canteen. We decided to cook rice and dal for those who were present with the help of the assistants. My past experience of such cooking at Ramnavami festival came handy. Not only our staff was supplied food but 8 /10 persons from the nearby LIC building with children were also fed. On that night one entire floor of Information Technology department headed by a lady officer was reserved for ladies as it was the most comfortable place in the bank. Most of us enjoyed sleeping on the respective tables. The ladies passed the night with some singing songs and some playing games. The next day morning again dawned with an incessant rains and strong Gail's. Somehow we arranged for black tea for those interested. Many ladies could not sleep because of not knowing about the well being of their kith and kin. The morning was sombre as nobody knew what would happen. There was no trace of any activity anywhere. Some staff went out for a stroll on Marine Drive but returned soon as it was raining heavily and because of strong windy conditions there were very high waves and hitting the barricade with a brute force. The only way out was wait and watch. We could not cook anything for the breakfast so distributed the biscuits only. We had no rice left in the kitchen so three of us and a sub staff went out on an errand to find out if any shop is open. There are mostly offices in the Nariman Point area. However, we could manage a bag full of rice from one of the hotels on credit, as the owner was known to our sub staff. We again cooked rice and dal but decided that now there would be rationing and only one serving as we may need Rice for the evening.

However the rainy conditions improved after 3 /4 pm and we got the information that buses may be plied though rail traffic was still closed. We arranged 4to 5 buses with the help of Mumbai Branch Manager and in two trips we shifted the staff to the nearby places. Making all the arrangement and for dispatching it took five /six hours and hence we stayed in the office the second night as we did not have any means of communication. We left next morning at about 8 am by the train which took 3 hours for a journey of 40 minutes.

Afterwards it came to the knowledge that at least 100 staff members had to suffer the loss of their goods, clothes and other belongings because the water had risen up to first floor in many areas.

This was a totally different experience in life. It enriched me and helped me to become a very acceptable person in CO.

Take Away

➢ **One should learn different arts of living.**

• • •

(4) A Tale of Two Executives

(I) Meeting with CMD

I was travelling to Mumbai from my present placement at a city branch; as a meeting was fixed between CMD of the bank, one Central Cabinet Minister and a State Government Minister for a difficult account of my branch. The account belonged to the company in which the State Government Minister had the controlling interest. The meeting was at 8pm but I had been called at 3 pm by the then CMD to get the first hand information about the status of the account. Since I was meeting the CMD for the first time there was a lot of pressure although I was well aware about the account and had taken all the backup papers.

I was called exactly at 3 pm in the CMD's cabin. I went inside with a pounding heart, but in minutes he made me absolutely comfortable. Then I explained him the views of the branch, what the company's demand was and what would be the possible solution and how far it would be fair for us to go down in our demand. He asked certain questions to get further insight in the case and the meeting ended. He asked me to be present for the meeting at 8 pm. He confirmed whether I am aware of the place.

The meeting began as scheduled and he put up the case in such a manner that it was a win-win situation for all. It was a great practical example for me how to put up the case before the high powered committee like that and to convince the other party tactfully.

The meeting was over at about 9.30 pm. CMD enquired how I would be reaching to the hotel, where I was boarding and should he give the lift as the meeting place was at a far off place.

Of course I thanked him and humbly told that I had made my own arrangement.

(II) A Visit by ZM

As scheduled our ZM was to visit our branch at 10 am for a Consortium Meeting at a sugar factory located at around 20 Km from the branch. The consortium meeting was at 2pm. Hence we had scheduled another visit to a famous religious place, the Trust was incidentaly our very good depositor. ZM reached exactly at 10 am. We welcomed him. After his initial review I suggested that we would go for a visit to the religious place and as a courtesy would meet the committee members of the Trust. He got infuriated and asked me who had fixed the schedule? On my explaining that it was done in consultation with the Secretary, he asked me who was the ZM? Sir, 'It was a protocol followed,' I answered. He became more irritated. In fact he had earlier asked several questions and verified the records with an auditor's eye, his earlier profession. We had satisfied all his queries and the development of the branch was also phenomenal as such he could not get any negative point and hence more irritation. Ultimately he agreed to visit the religious place, never the less he did not fail to comment that the business and religion should not be mixed. I informed him that the place we would be going was invariably visited by one and all personalities who go to the city right from The President of India. He did not comment on it but was reluctant as clearly reflected from his body language. We reached the place, then I told him to remove shoes and cover the head with a scarf. He was looking at me in great anger. I told him that it was a protocol to be followed religiously and I went to do the needful. Several people were there and hence he had no other go than to follow. But when we reached that sacred place it had the magnetic effect and now he was looking with the wide eyes the sheer beauty and the holiness of the place. The serenity of the place had made him silent with content. Then we visited the Committee Office and as per their practice they honoured him with a Turban and other artifact. On way back, he did not utter a word.

We returned to the branch by 1pm, where the MD of the sugar mill was waiting for us. I introduced our ZM to the MD, he invited the ZM to join him, so that all of us would go to the Sugar Mill in their AC Vehicle and would join for lunch there. ZM declined. Although the MD requested to accompany as it was a very hot month in summer and the road was dusty and very rough. Still ZM insisted that he would use his Car and told us to go ahead. We reached by 1.30 pm but there was no trace of the other Car. MD told his driver to retrace the ZM. He came back along with them at around 3 pm. Our ZM was absolutely disturbed as their vehicle had a flat tyre. He had dusty clothes, he was late for the meeting, was hungry and had to use company vehicle. On arrival it was suggested that we would have the lunch and would start the meet at 4 pm as none of us had taken the lunch. NO- no, first meeting was his order.

Somehow we finished the meeting and returned at branch. I had then arranged sumptuous snacks, which he consumed. He immediately started at about 5.30pm for another branch where I accompanied him to show the road. No conversion took place for about 15 minutes on the way. He reluctantly shook hands and left with a wry smile.

Take Away :

These two incidents took place in a span of one month. But what a stark difference?

➢ **One was patient, magnanimous, considerate, had courtesy and a knack to handle the situation tactfully.**

➢ **It was learning how to make your sub ordinate comfortable.**

➢ **It was a lesson for unlearning.**

4 | WOW FROM THE CUSTOMERS!

Vow

by an International Bank!

We are committed to making banking easy

1. We will extend our opening hours in our busiest branches.
2. We will aim to serve the majority of customers within 5 minutes in our branches.
3. We will provide you with friendly, helpful service whenever you deal with us.

   We're aiming to get 9 out of 10 customers to rate our service as helpful.
4. We will help you to make the right choices for you and your money.

   All of our branch literature will be simplified and rewritten in line with customer feedback. We will also introduce a new Customer Service programe.
5. We will provide a 24/7 telephone banking service.

   Our call centers will give you the option to speak to a real person.

   We are committed to helping when you need us
6. We are committed to keeping you safe online.

7. We will help you quickly if your debit card is lost or stolen and you need access to cash.

8. We will continue to be a responsible lender and are committed to finding new ways to help.

   We are committed to supporting the communities we work in

9. We pledge to stay open for business if we are the last bank in town and will consider a range of options to ensure a local banking service is available.

10. We will teach over 25,000 financial education lessons in schools in 20...

11. We will actively support the local community in which we live and work.

    We are committed to listening

12. We will resolve customer complaints fairly, consistently, and promptly.

    We are aiming for 75% of customers to be satisfied with the way their complaint has been handled.

13. Twice a year we will publish the most common of complaints.

14. We will actively seek your thoughts and suggestions on how we can become more helpful.

Sounds good.

We don't expect to achieve all of them immediately, and we know that we have work to do, but we will be open about our progress.

• • •

(1) Bohani! (The First Big Business Deal)

It was a Saturday and being a half day we were preparing to close down, it was already 4.30 pm. All the staff members except my colleague Shri Sunil had already left the Branch office. We were putting down the shutter at that moment the telephone rang. We pushed back the half opened shutter and attended the phone. The phone was from Mr. Anoopbhai, Manager of one of our best clients. He was enquiring whether we were in the branch as he wanted very urgently a Demand Draft (DD) for Rs. 35 lakhs. Shri Sunil responded that we will come back in five minutes since all accounts and the system were already closed at around 2 pm. We were pondering on the matter, then we again received a call now from Shri Praveenbhai the M.D. of the Company, he told that the DD is required urgently as the same was to be deposited with State Government tomorrow at Guwahati and he is sending his representative to Mumbai to catch late night flight at around 2 am I could perceive the anxiety in his voice. Travel time from Pune to Mumbai was around four hours.

We decided to call back our Head Cashier and another officer who were holding the keys of the lockers. However Head Cashier had left Pune and was around 30 Kms. away. The other officer carrying the keys could not be contacted he was also out of station for Pooja.

Sunil and I tried various other branches for getting some assistance but it was in fructuous. In the mean time we called back our Daftari Shri Sada who was staying nearby. The representative of our client was already there. We reopened the day in the Computer system since at that time no present facilities of CBS (Centralized Banking Solution) was in vogue. Similarly the RTGS, NEFT and Net Banking facilities were yet to arrive then. Even the Mobile Phones were an exquisite luxury item only available with exceptional HNI clients.

In the meantime Sunil with his usual style arranged for presence of one of our CTO's (Computer Terminal Operator) for data entry and to process the issuance of DD. But where were the DD leaves? Our Daftari Shri Sada told that few remaining leaves at the end of the day were stored in the safe box in the Godrej Store well kept outside the strong room. But again the keys were in the safe.

It was already 6 pm and time was running out. We, Sunil and myself discussed the issue and ultimately decided to call a Key maker to open the store-well. We sent our Daftari on this errand. He came back in half an hour along with the Key Master. He was not agreeable to open since it was Bank's property. We showed him our Identity Cards and gave a letter of authority to him in Rajbhasha to prepare duplicate keys and open the Store-well and Box. He deftly completed the job in no time. We could get the remaining 4/5 DD leaves and the necessary steps were taken for issuance of DD.

All said and done with all these efforts we could ultimately prepare and hand over the requisite DD's to the client at around 8 pm. He immediately proceeded to Mumbai to catch 2 am flight.

After this incidence on 3rd or 4th day I was entering the branch at around 10 am when Sunil greeted me with his usual beaming smile and informed that Shri Praveen Seth the MD of the company was waiting for me. On reaching my cabin Shri Praveenbhai hugged me. He informed that the DD was the Tender Money; thereby they could get an order of Rs40 Crores from the Government. This tender had a special value as it was a 'Mahurat' tender and thereby an auspicious beginning 'A BOHANI' at the beginning of the year was struck.

He was all praise for the staff, since he was fully narrated by his Manager, the efforts taken by the branch staff.

It was a team effort, though we had transgressed the usual banking practice a bit. It was done for the renowned client for the just cause. Of course my all vigilant colleague Shri Sunil informed the whole incident to our Regional Office next day.

I may add that our client had a turnover of over Rs.300 Crores and we never faced any problem to surpass targets given to us.

We had won the heart of an HNI client for our Bank who will forever stay with us!

Take away :

➢ **What will differentiate a winner from others will be the value creation for the customer.**

> ➤ **If a customer makes a request for something special, do everything you can, to say yes!**

• • •

(2) Recognition

My colleague Mr. Hemant was handling Savings Deposit counter and if I recollect correctly it was November 1973. Diwali was on the corner as such there was an atmosphere of festivities. There were about 15 ledgers of Savings Account holders of very large size to be managed.

Then the system of withdrawl from savings account was that customer would give duly filled in withdrawal form and the passbook to the ledger keeper. In turn he would get a metal token to be exchanged for cash at cash counter.

Ledger keeper would post the withdrawl form in the account, make the entries in the passbook which would then be directed to the cash department along with payment scroll. SB counter would always be surrounded by many customers. On that day too several customers were being attended by Mr. Hemant and a middle aged customer was one of them. The customer furnished the withdrawal form and his passbook to Mr. Hemant who deftly sent it to paying cashier. The customer collected the cash and returned to the savings bank counter, somehow he reached Mr. Hemant took out a Five Rupee note and gave it to Mr.Hemant. Hemant was so awed by such an action that he took it in his hand. Totally perplexed he was simultaneously looking towards the customer and the note with a confused look. Customer smiled and showing the passbook to other customers standing nearby, exclaimed, 'What a wonderful handwriting and the way of writing entries gentleman!' I am really delighted, thank you.

Then Rs. 5 was a valuable sum as a cup of tea was costing paisa 25.

Any way it was not the prize that mattered but the spontaneous WOW of the customer! Of course Mr. Hemant very humbly returned the note with thanks and told that his reorganization itself is the real prize!

Take Away :
> **Most of the Customers are satisfied if very simple and basic needs are satiated.**

• • •

(3) How to win a Customer?

My staff member Shri Himanshu entered the cabin accompanying a person and introduced to me, 'Sir, meet Mr. Arvind Patel,' he is running a furniture shop in the market for last 25 years. We exchanged greetings.

Shri Himanshu further told that Mr. Patel had a daughter and a son who was already been admitted in one of the premier Universities in California, USA for a Post Graduation degree and left India 2 weeks back. Their father desired that they should bear the expenses for studying abroad as it helps to create the responsible student. They also were of the same opinion as informed by Mr. Arvindbhai and hence decided to avail Educational loans to the tune of Rs15 lakhs each. Mr. Arvindbhai approached his banker SBI. However the bank had not shown any interest as the students were already abroad. He further informed that Mr. Himanshu knows him well and incidentally understood the requirement. He assured Mr. Arvindbhai that it will be taken care of by our branch.

I was always a team man and had an innate love for teaching. I had developed a knack to sensitize my staff to be always on the lookout for good viable opportunities, activities, proposals on asset as well as liability side and for other ancillary services. Mr. Himanshu also informed that the students had an offer from two different Universities and hence decided to choose the one only after reaching USA and hence not applied for any Education Loan before leaving India. He further added that Mr. Arvindbhai was a good friend of his father and therefore he had assured him that our branch would take care of his requirement.

While discussing the proposal we gathered that he and his wife owned two residential flats in one of the posh areas of the city. He was having a good luxury car, joint investments to the tune of over Rs.25 lakhs, Insurance policies of substantial value and fixes deposits of Rs 30 lakhs.

His savings bank accounts were also having fat balances. He was and is a treasurer of one of the famous Jain temples in the city. He maintains a Current account of his proprietorship firm in SBI and there also transactions were satisfactory.

Mr. Himanshu also told me that he is a person of repute. On understanding and estimating the risk and reward I approved the proposal in principle. Shri Arvindbhai seems to be awed because of the quick decision while Mr. Himanshu was all smiles as his word was respected.

I briefed my staff to collect all necessary documents from Shri Arvindbhai, to carry out normal inspection and put up the proposals to me for usual formal sanction. Shri Himanshu was so enthused that the proposals were put up for sanction within 2 days. We handed over sanction letters on third day. On our behalf we requested Shri Arvindbhai to open a joint Savings account of himself and his wife who would be the Guarantor for the proposed loans. Shri Arvindbhai began the account with initial deposit of Rs.1 lakh and further requested us to open two different Savings accounts in the name of the students wherein he would deposit Rs 50,000/- each. He had a special request to urgently remit US $ 3000 (approximately equal to Rs.1.45 lakhs) from each loan account as entry fees as given in the schedule of fees. My accountant was little shaky as formalities of Loan Documentation was not complete. I instructed him to prepare two sets of documents duly stamped and get them executed by Mr. Arvindbhai, the two Guarantee documents by Mrs. Chandrikaben, wife of Mr. Arvindbhai. In the mean time the sanction letters were mailed to Mr.Tushar the son and Miss Jyoti the daughter to scan back the same with acceptance of not only the terms and conditions but also authority to open loan accounts and to disburse the amount before executing the Loan documents which they would execute and send back. Also an authority letter from both duly drafted to complete all necessary formalities for loan by their father.

A letter was also mailed to The Director Administration of the University requesting that he would help the students to get loan documents executed before The Indian Consulate, situated in the city. The students arranged an affirmation from the Director Administration and mail was received next day. This mail was not only a confirmation of admission but also would ensure completion of the legal process of loan documentation.

Our Loan department was instructed to put up the suitable note incorporating all these details; it was then approved by me (being the Branch Manager). The requisite DD's in US $ 3000 were obtained from Forex dealing branch by recovering margin amounts and disbursing loan amounts. A request letter addressed to The Director Administration ....University was prepared thanking him for his cooperation and further requesting him to arrange for due completion of the formalities of enclosed documents. The places to be signed were pencil marked. A draft copy of confirmation for execution of documents by The Consulate was also sent for reference. A self addressed cloth bound Envelope was also dispatched along with Loan Documents, Loan Application forms, Saving Account application forms etc. to The Director Administration ...... The complete set duly executed was received back in a period of about three to four weeks and our accountant was relived of tension.

It was but obvious that Mr. Arvindbhai transferred his Current Account to our branch and gifted us with huge deposits of over Rs.1.5 Crores of the Jain Temple. He also mobilized several other accounts of his friends, and became a Marketing person for all products and ancillary services such as life and non life policies, credit cards and even Loan Products.

During the visit of Regional Manager Mr. Himanshu was felicitated.

This is the way to clinch a customer!

Take Away :
> **If we do not take care of our customers then someone else will.**

➤ **Flexibility**

Customers want the Manager to 'jiggle' the system to make it work for them.
They don't want to hear 'No.'

➤ **Employee Relationship :** Treat them that they are your important resource.
Train them to handle different situations.

➤ **Use the Motivators :** Give them challenging tasks, responsibility and guidance. Recognize them for their achievement or completing the job successfully.

• • •

(4) Gas Connection

It was a very busy day; I had just finished off the papers lying before me and was enjoying a cup of tea. The Head Peon of the branch came in with an unknown person, dressed nicely. I welcomed him with a smile and offered a chair; a cup of tea was also brought-in for the guest. He himself introduced to me as Doctor Dongre. He was employed with CRPF and their camp was located at an approximate distance of 25 Km. from our city branch. His earlier posting was at Jaipur and in this place he had joined the duties this morning only. He had to purchase certain household items and hence visited the city. He was the account holder of our bank at Jaipur and dropped-in as he had seen Central Bank's board. During the discussion I gathered that he belonged to Nagpur which incidentally is also my native place. We had some common acquaintances and college friends as reveled during our discussion. He shown intention to open his account, at that time his wife joined him and enquired about a safe deposit locker. The doctor informed that presently no documents are in his possession, but only remember his SB account number maintained at Chandpole Gate, Jaipur branch. In those days introduction had more importance, but he did not know anybody in the city. At that time the CBS system was also not there. On the basis of interaction I was convinced, hence using my discretionary power I allowed SB department to open the account as well as issued a locker. Of course in the mean time I had faxed the signatures of the couple to our Chandpole Gate, Jaipur branch for confirmation which arrived by the evening. Doctor as well his wife was very happy as one of his requirements was completed seamlessly. Another client also had some urgent work with me as such I focussed my attention to him seeking excuse for a moment from the Doctor. When I was attending to the other client I overheard that Doctor was in need of a Gas connection. After disposal of the matter on hand, I asked the couple how I could be of their help. Doctor informed that in fact his errand to the city was for a Gas Connection and asked for help. I called my peon and told him to accompany them to nearby M/S Sai Services as Doctor was new to the city. I spoke with the proprietor Shri Chavan of the Gas Agency and requested him to help the Doctor.

It so happened that my SB officer Mr. Rahatikar had met with an accident & lost his right leg. He was a very competent officer & backbone of operations department in the branch despite his handicap. Mr. Chavan owner of M/S Sai Gas Agency had also met with an accident and his hands were amputed. Mr. Rahatiker & Mr. Chavan were operated at the same Nursing home & had developed the friendship. Mr. Rahatikar was instrumental in canvassing the account of M/S Sai Gas Agency. We used to give door step service right from opening of account to Shri Chavan since he was physically challenged.

When I took over the charge of the branch I observed that every day Mr. Rahatikar had a tough time maneuvering the steep 4/5 flights. Urgently a ramp and a strong suitable railing was built and steps repaired. This had also facilitated the aged clients and Mr. Chavan. These small gestures play vital role in improvement in services and hence the business.

Soon I received a call from the doctor; he was all praise for facilitating the gas connection. Doctor transferred a fixed deposit of Rs 25 lacs from other bank during next three months.

Take Away :

➤ All the Banking Products can be easily cloned. It means that your only Real Competitive edge is your relations with Staff. And in turn staff relationship with your Customers.

➤ This is one thing which your Competitors cannot steal from you.

• • •

(5) Moments of Truth

This is Ravi speaking, hello Gokhaleji, 'I am at Japan and it is 2 am as per local time in Tokyo'. The voice had a concern. I greeted Mr. Ravi and asked why he is so much bothered? He was bang straight to the point, 'Shri Mohan of M/S Jay Industry who are our suppliers for last 10 years informed that a small Cheque of Rs 21 lakhs was dishonored by Central Bank of India. This is perhaps the first time our cheque is returned in last 30 years and as such I am perturbed.' I replied that I do not think having returned any cheque; however please furnish telephone no. of Shri Mohan. It was given, I assured Mr. Ravi that I will look personally in the matter and there may be some misunderstanding. It may be added that Mr. Ravi was CMD of the company M/S Ravi Oils Ltd., dealing with our bank for over 30 years and their annual turnover was over Rs1,000 Crores.

At the first hand we verified all records at our office, then at clearing house member branch, but there was no record of return of cheque. I put up a call to Shri Mohan of M/S Jay Industry, on enquiring it was gathered that he had deposited the cheque in their bank Corporation Bank at Delhi. To obtain full information I requested him to furnish Telephone no of the bank. On speaking with them it was found that Cheque was returned by Central Bank of India, Delhi and reason was that it was not drawn on them, but was drawn on and payable at Pune. At that time branches were not connected through CBS and multi city cheque facility also was not available. Thus it was not the mistake at our bank end; in fact the Corporation Bank had lodged it in Delhi clearing instead of sending it under collection at Pune. This information was communicated to the Finance Manager of the Company, since it was odd hours at Tokyo.

Next I telephoned back to Mr. Mohan seeking from him the information about the nearest Branch of Central Bank of India and asked how if I pay him by bankers cheque and that too on the very day? He informed that their banker telephoned him confirming that it was the mistake of Corporation Bank. Then a telephone call was put up to our Branch at Chandani Chowk Delhi. We first narrated the whole story to the said Branch Manager. Informed how valuable the said Company was to our Bank. Further informing that every day we remit TT (Telegraphic Transfer) for this company. Branch Manager agreed to issue and keep ready the Bankers' Cheque favouring M/S Jay Industries. We through a fax communicated the said message to the branch authorizing them to raise a debit to account (M/S Ravi Oils Ltd) entry through a manifold. The said entry was responded through a return fax.

In the mean time Mr. Mohan was requested to call on at our Delhi branch with the returned cheque. The Branch Manager at Delhi welcomed Mr. Mohan and promptly did his part of the job.

Mr. Mohan telephoned me from there only; he could not hide a shade of **dismay** from his voice and further very happily asked me what he should do besides informing to the Company officials and Mr. Ravi. I may quote what he said next, 'I had never come across a banker who cares so much about their customers, I would be delighted to meet you in person during my next visit to Pune, thank you.'

I requested him to open a Current Account at Delhi office, he laughed and said done. Next day I received a thanks giving call from Delhi Branch Manager.

I received a telephone call from Singapore from of course Mr. Ravi, not only giving thanks', now his voice was very warm, clearly reflecting **a WOW!**

Next day Mr. Ravi visited the branch with a Bouquet, he hugged me, his smile contained everything what a Branch Manager could imagine!

'Sir, thank you, it is the result of the team efforts of the staff members working at our two branches.' I said with a smile.

Take Away :

➢ **Banking is not just deposits, advances but in reality it is creating faith and confidence in the minds of their customers!**

➢ **A Bank Manager should always have a professional approach!**

➢ **Build Rapport, unite with the customer in addressing the problem: 'Let's see what we can do to resolve this issue.'**

● ● ●

(6) Remote Sensing

That day was a bit non busy day and after finishing the lunch I was looking for some old circulars to decide settlement of a deceased claim. A phone call was there from one of our reputed clients Mr. Ashishbhai, an iron and steel merchant. He had all his accounts with us and the entire turnover of about Rs.15 Crores was enrouted through his accounts. He had called me to check whether I was in the branch and within half an hour or so he was there in the branch.

He straight way touched the subject as per his usual style. Sir, 'One of my relatives Shri Shyamlal, an agriculturist, stays at a village Rampur which was about 45 Kms from the district place Mandsoor in Madhaya Pradesh(M.P.). Mr. Shyamlal had a daughter and she was selected for the course of MBA in Narsi Monji Institute, a reputed Educational Institution in Mumbai. Mr. Shyamlal desired that an Educational Loan be raised urgently, as Rs4.50 lakhs out of the total expenses of Rs12 lakhs were to be remitted to the Institution within a week. There was no bank in their village but only a Post Office. Our branch was in Pune, Maharashtra, about 1000 Kms away.

Shri Shyamlal was a literate agriculturist. The monsoons had set in and since lot of money was already spent on agricultural operations he was unable to raise that much money, hence need the Loan. He further told that the student had to report to the Institution within 7 days and it requires about 2 days to reach Mumbai from their village as such she would have to go directly to Mumbai. On completion he stopped. I said that means I had only a day in my hand to decide and act. He smiled.

Imagine the situation that there was no document on my hand, the loan was to be given to the persons with whom I had never met; it was to be given to a student staying out of command area of the branch. The communication facilities as Mobile phones, E mails etc.(Period 1998-99) were not so common. Against all odds only one straw was reputation, worth and long association of over 30 years of my client and the value of his guarantee. These aspects outweighed the risks and hence I took the decision then and there only to go ahead. Mr. Ashishbhai was pleased with my decision.

I got the details of the student, father and a fax copy of the letter from Narsee Monji Institute, Mumbai confirming the admission of Miss Reema Lakhotia for two years MBA course. I gave him an application form and told him to fill in the same to the extent possible and bring it tomorrow. I also furnished other documents i.e. Asset, Liability declarations to be filled in likewise for the applicants and him. He gave me a blank cheque for the expenses to be incurred and left.

Now I had to act fast and undertake various steps. First I checked the Stamp Duty in the two States, it was higher in Maharashtra. I deputed my Clark, who was well versed with the documentation work, as mentored by me, to complete the requisite set of documents duly stamped. Then I got the telephone number of the Post Office at Rampur and spoke with the Post Master after giving my introduction. I enquired about Shri Shyamlal Lakhotia. He immediately responded that Shri Shyamlalji was a person of repute, he was a progressive agriculturist and had over 50 acres of good fertile land, he further told that he had substantial amount of NSC's at the Post Office. He furthered that his beti (daughter), Reema was a very talented and the only merit student of the district. I noted all this information as a part of market report. I informed him that I may extend an Education Loan to the student but a letter of introduction and verification of signature would be required from him. He happily agreed but requested to dictate the format. He did give the same along with photographs pasted on it. In those days the PAN, Aadhar cards were not in vogue.

I had observed that whenever you help others and that too without any vested interest all the doors for help automatically open for you too!

Next I telephoned to the Branch Manager of our Bank at Mandsoor. After my introduction he appeared to be a responsive BM. I Explained to him all the details about Shri Shyamlalji Lakhotia, his daughter Miss Rema and the Education Loan I had sanctioned. I requested him to help me. I further informed him that Lakhotias would be calling on him within 2 to 3 days for executing the documents for Loan. He would be sending the executed documents to me by Registered post. His obvious question was how he would recognize Lakhotias? I told him about the introduction letter from Post Office. The BM informed that he had never executed Education Loan Documents. On this I explained that all relevant places meant for signatures would be marked as 'X' and even the Proforma letter of execution to be sent by him would be enclosed and a self addressed Cloth bound envelope would also be sent for returning the executed documents to our branch.

Having done all the ground work, next day morning I was waiting for Mr. Ashishbhai, he arrived, handed over the documents partly completed and after discussion he suggested that he would be sending a person to Rampur this evening so that the things would move fast. The envelopes containing all the documents were handed over to Mr. Ashishbhai.

On third day I received a telephone call from our Branch Manager that Lakhotias were there, he had completed all the documents and his certificate of execution was also ready. I requested him to fax it to me after putting his Signature Index Number. He had completed his job and happily informed me that Shri Lakhotia had assured him to give a fresh deposit of Rs 1 lac after harvest.

I received the Fax, got a Guarantee executed from Mr. Ashishbhai, opened the Loan account, disbursed the amount and handed the DD favouring Narsee Monji Institute towards fees to Mr. Ashishbhai. He was very happy and satisfied having done his job in a professional way.

We received the documents in a week's time. In due course Miss Rema earned the MBA degree and got a good job. She repaid the loan in the course of time. Though I had no opportunity to meet her at any time my best wishes to her! Mr. Ashishbhai brought a good savings account of a Jain organization and at least 5 to 6 current accounts. Through him a tie up with a reputed builder was made and thereby about 12 very good Housing loan accounts could be disbursed. He became our Marketing Manager.

Take Away :

➢ Remember banking is faith and a banker must be able to identify a genuine customer.

➢ He should make the independent enquires about the prospective borrower.

➢ Always create a record of the attempt you had made to understand the borrower.

➢ If you had to take help from a person at a remote place, create confidence in him and guide him.

• • •

<u>Remember</u>

➢ **The products and services are easily cloned in commodities and services spheres.**

➢ **A bank can differentiate itself from its competitors only through its customer service.**

- If we do not take care of our customers then someone else will.
- The Next Generation Banking is going to be full of business opportunities in terms of volumes but tough on margins due to fierce competition.
- Gen Next Banks will have to provide basic banking services to their customers with speed and efficiency which is a minimum must.
- What will differentiate a winner from others will be the value creation for the customer.
- Today the customer is more knowledgeable, demanding, analytical and aware of his rights.
- It is therefore a challenging task before the banking sector to revisit their entire working modules, up gradation of skills, technology, and policies so that they are competent to withstand the international competitive environment.

(Source I I B F Bulletin)

• • •

What Customers Want?

The delightful dozen!

The most critical needs are :

1. They want to see efforts.
2. They want to have options.
3. They want to be understood.
4. They expect speedy service, especially when they are in a hurry.
5. They are sensitive to confidentiality.
6. They want to be seen as important.
7. They like positive surprises.
8. They want their needs to be satisfied.
9. They want value for money, not just a cheap service.
10. They like simplicity and can't be bothered to understand the complexity of our service or products.

11. They want to be treated consistently and fairly, especially in comparison with other customers.
12. They like reliable service in order to make better decisions.

(Source I I B F Bulletin)

• • •

Introspect !

A study conducted on causes for Customer Defection and Loss of Customers in Banks, the following reasons have been identified.

Rate the reasons as perceived by you. : On a Scale of 1 to 9.

- 1. Lured by competition.
- 2. Product dissatisfaction.
- 3. Courting other brands.
- 4. High transaction cost and service charges.
- 5. Death of customer.
- 6. Moving out of town.
- 7. Preference for better delivery channels.
- 8. Preference for better and cosier service outlets.
- 9. Attitude of indifference by the staff.

Nine is One

(Source I I B F Bulliten)

• • •

Reaserch has Proved!

'Customers do not select the bank for the catchy slogans and colourful brochures, but for the efficient and prompt service offered to them, creating faith and confidence in the minds of their customers!'

5 | SOCIAL ENGINEERING

(1) Employment

It really was a very hectic day, since last two days were Public holidays. Everybody in the branch was looking for closing down the day's activities. Cash transactions were closed at around 5.30 pm. Head cashier along with other cash officer after counting cash, closed the doors of the safe and returned to their chairs. Shri Sunil, our staff came in my cabin with a youth and introduced him as Mr. Ramesh. He has requested to issue a Demand Draft, to be attached along with the application for employment. Mr. Ramesh further informed that the relevant application form itself was received very late and today was the last day of the remittance. He had earlier tried with two banks but was refused and thereafter he came to our branch as a last resort. The boy appeared to be honest. Mr Sunil suggested that though cash transaction was closed we can issue a DD by transfer transaction. Since Mr. Ramesh was not having any account in our bank, I instantly took out and gave the cheque from my account to make the DD. The boy was beaming with the joy when DD was in his hand. He left the branch thanking me and giving me DD amount of Rs.350/- in cash.

During the last week (March 2015) only, I met Shri Sunil and he reminded me about the story. He further told that Mr.Ramesh is now our proud customer, who remembers the incident and always says, 'But for that DD from Central Bank Of

India, I would not have been in the present prestigious employment.'

Take Away :

> ➤ **Extend a little help which is always within your power, this gives an immense satisfaction.**

• • •

(2) Free Lance Marketing Officer

I t was 10.15 am and all of us had gathered together for our usual morning prayer when a lady came inside from the front door beaming at us. I recognized her and with a gesture told her to join us in the prayers. After completing the prayer she showed her intent to speak, and I gave my assent. She began -

"I am Miss Sujata, now a proud Chartered Accountant. I have pleasure to inform all of you that results of final ICA was declared yesterday and I stood 2'nd in the Merit list. The entire credit of my success goes to Shri Gokhale sahib and customer of Central Bank of India, Shri Gopalbhai. I request all of you to enjoy the sweets and she bowed to me." I was literally moved by her performance and the gesture shown by her.

My staff welcomed and cheered us by thunderous clapping and then came the demand from a staff member to let them hear the entire story. All other staff members then joined in a chorus supporting the demand. I may add that after the prayer it was our routine at R.O. to exchange the important instructions, circulars, happenings by one or two staff members.

I began narrating, "It was perhaps 3 pm when a peon informed that there is a lady desirous to meet me and is asking permission to come in. I allowed her. But lots of customers kept me continuously engaged up to 5 pm. She was patiently waiting, for the cabin to be vacant. Then she came in and stood. She sat only after I offered her a seat. There was a sign of stress on her face but despite that she smiled and introduced her as Miss Sujata Soni. Sir, I am a student pursuing Chartered Accountancy. I have recently cleared Intermediate examination for C A and now preparing for the Final CA Examination which would be conducted after about 10 months. I congratulated her! In the mean time one of our respected customers Shri Gopalbhai came in and sat on the sofa kept at the back side of the cabin. I gave a welcome smile and with a gesture requested to sit. He also communicated by gesture that he is not in a hurry and would wait. She continued, I am presently an article with one of the Chartered Accountant firms and is paid a monthly stipend of Rs. 2000/-. Since I have already completed the requisite period of internship, I desire to fully concentrate on my final year studies. I interrupted by questioning, how am I in the picture? and asked further what her parents are doing? She was totally unknown to me and we were meeting for the first time. She furthered, Sir my father is no more, my mother is a cook and I have a younger sister who is studying in a school. Our family is solely dependent on the said source of income. I am visiting you for some help so that I need not have to go on duties and could fully concentrate on my studies as I cannot afford to reappear."

On patiently listening and thinking for a moment, I could not fit her requirement in any of the banks' loan scheme. I instantly took out my cheque book and through my sub staff drew Rs8, 000/ -from my account and gave it to her. She was literally in tears. I assured her that this would take care of your financial requirement for the time being and in a month or so I would arrange for rest of the amount. I may add that my mother was bedridden at my native place and I was remitting about Rs. 25,000/- per month required for her nursing. Miss Sujata had no words and while sitting there her face could communicate a sense of gratitude.

At that moment Shri Gopalbhai got up and sat beside her, all this time he had been a passive listener. Miss Sujata started to get up, Shri Gopalbhai asked her to sit for a moment. He slowly drew out a cheque book from his pocket,signed the cheque and handed over to her saying, 'Beti Yeh apke nanaji ke tarafse hai ! Jitne chaho utni rashi likh lena,mera aashirwad hai! Lekin mithai dena nahi bhulana!'

She started sobbing! Then we pacified her by giving a glass of water. She thanked us, bowed down and went away!

After her departure Shri Gopalbhai in a very husky voice said, Shri Gokhaleji you have given me two things, one is a lesson how to fulfill our obligations towards the society by helping a really needy person and secondly an opportunity to serve. I do not have words to thank you!

Shri Gopalbhai was our High Net Worth, N R I client always maintaining a balance of over Rs150 lacs in his Savings account.

I would always be ready to help if you give me such an opportunity! He very warmly hugged me took my hand in his and left!

Miss Sujata had drawn only Rs18,000/- from the account. After 3 months I was transferred to Rajkot as Regional Manager and now I am with you!" There was a thunderous applaud again by my staff!

Then Miss Sujata thanked me, saluted me and said now I am a Proud Customer of Central Bank of India, ...Branch and assure you that I will be a life time **Free Lance Marketing Officer** of the Bank.

Take Away :

➢ **Never fritter away the chance you get to help others.**

➢ **It may be that almighty has chosen you for this sacred deed.**

➢ **Remember the law of nature, every good action will come back to you with bonus.**

➢ **By your good deeds your Institution will also gain.**

• • •

(3) The Surgery

'Hello Sir, this is Govind speaking, did you recognize?' Are you from despatch department? Yes Sir. The voice was reflecting not only the emergency but also that the speaker was under great pressure. I was then working at Central Staff Department (CSD), Central Office, Mumbai.

The department undertakes all the necessary administrative requirements of the staff right from CMD to a Lift Operator in respect of their Salary/Wages, Leave, Medical Bills, LFC, TA bills, Loans, Transfers up to scale III officers etc. There were around 1600 staff members coming under the jurisdiction of CSD.

I asked Shri Govind to calm down and tell me what has happened? He told hurriedly that Mr. Sampat of my department while crossing road met with an accident, there was a head injury and he was bleeding but fully conscious. I immediately told him to take him to the nearby Government Hospital - The J J Hospital. I further told him that I would also be reaching there as fast as possible. I first called my Senior Manager and briefed him the steps to be taken. First was to find out the blood group, inform to 3 to 4 donors from our list that there was an emergency and they should be ready. Second to inform about the accident to some responsible person from his family, Third inform the department in charge and DGM (HRD) and Security In-charge, Fourth to arrange some cash, Fifth not to keep his Mobile engaged. Then I proceeded along with our Daftari to the said hospital as he had some relations working in the hospital and an officer colleague Shri Abhay.

When I reached the Emergency Ward Shri Govind was relived he was attending the usual formalities of admission required in any Government Hospital. Mr. Sampat was lying on a stretcher profusely bleeding. Some Internee doctor was attending to him; I was also scared as the blood was oozing out.

I was then new to Mumbai and did not have many contacts. I was so engrossed in thinking, how an urgent attendance of a senior doctor could be arranged. In the mean time a lady doctor was keenly looking at me but I was totally unaware. She only called me, Gokhale Sir did you not recognize me? Still I was at loss, she only asked me Sir, 'I am Janki from Nanded', and bowed to pay respect, a light glowed in my mind and I went 10 years back. Are you Janki Chavan ? She smilingly told yes Sir, now I am Dr. Janki, M. S., and in charge of Surgery Department. What is the matter and who is this patient? I narrated her in few words and vow! The wheels started moving and in no time Shri Sampat was not only admitted but was taken for surgery in the concerned operation theatre to be attended by Dr. Janki. In the mean time my Senior Manager had managed for two donors and he was also there. The elder brother of Mr. Sampat also joined us. It was informed by the Intern doctor that it may take about 2 to 3 hours for the entire operation and in the mean time Dr. Janki had asked him to arrange for tea in her cabin.

We were sitting in the cozy cabin of Dr. Janki when our officer colleague Mr. Abhay was all the way looking with awe! Contemplating how things moved so fast like a magical wand when the fairy in the form of Dr. Janki appeared! He was very anxious to know my relationship with her and perused me to tell the same as substantial time was available with us. We had played our role.

My narration followed,

'I had joined our Nanded branch only a week ago and was invited by the Secretary, Rotary Club Nanded for their annual function. Many other bankers and reputed personalities of the city were present. The hall was packed to its capacity of around 250. Amongst other felicitations one was for scholar students. At that time they called Ms Janki and her father, since she stood 9th in the merit list for the 12th examination. She was given a prize and a bouquet to her father. He was wearing a crumpled shirt reflecting his poverty. He in his modest language thanked the club but further said with an anguish that, 'My daughter is admitted in the Government college but I doubt whether she will be able to become a doctor as I am unable to meet her educational expenses.' These words had such an impact on me that I immediately raised my hand, seeking permission from the Chairman to speak, as protocol demanded. He permitted and requested me to come up and introduce also as I was very new to the city. I began with thanks to Rotary to invite me and permit me to speak. I introduced myself as Branch Manager of Central Bank Of India a leading Nationalised bank and declared that my Central Bank Of India would bear all the Educational expenses of Miss Janki. Such was the impact that, for a while all eyes were focussed on me and then a loud applause followed. I was sure that henceforth my Bank would be recognized in the business circle and as such the brand name of the bank was perfectly marketed.

Next day the father and Ms Janaki visited the branch; her father was a rickshaw puller and was illiterate. They had a small one room house which was about 12 Km. from city and a total of 6 persons were staying there in. My loan department staff was kind enough to complete the formalities and they disbursed the loan as per sanction norms. However while sanctioning the loan I had slightly tweaked the rules and had sanctioned an additional loan amount for the hostel accommodation although it was then not allowed as she was staying in the same place. Yes, as expected a query was raised by Regional Office on the above matter, seeking my explanation.

My answer was, please refer to Point No 15 incorporated in my sanction, it reads, "As a special case the facility of Hostel fees was allowed, taking into the consideration the following two aspects. (i) As the student stays at a distance of about 12 km from city and would require to spend Rs. 20/- per day for her commutation. (ii) There are 6 persons staying in a single room where a budding lady doctor will have to stay and she would not be able to concentrate on her studies.

No further query was raised.

I used to celebrate an annual function of the branch /office where ever I worked. For Nanded branch also I started such a function. We had then invited our Zonal Manager as a Chief Guest, along with Regional Manager and local customers and noncustomers. It was a strong congregation of about 200 odd people. Felicitation of Merit Candidates was a part of the Function. Of course Miss Janki was also a winner. One of our staff introduced her in the function to the dignitaries as a budding doctor. She happily told that, she was thankful to Shri Gokhale Sir and Central Bank Of India as without their support she would not have been studying Medicine. She declared that in the First Year Exam she stood 2nd in the merit list. One and all applauded her. Our Regional Manager stood up out of turn and before the gathering and ZM applauded me, after describing the fact of calling an explanation from me. Not only he sought excuse from me, but further said our bank will only prosper if such a pragmatic and out of box thinking Managers are there. Of course Zonal Manager was also equally impressed and said encouraging words."

On completion of my submission Mr. Abhay said that, Sir after these two functions it is but obvious that, you and your Branch must had been **A Star Performer**.

I had just completed, when Dr. Janki entered with an assured smile on her face which was speaking that the surgery was successful and Mr. Sampat was all **right.**

All of us departed happily after heartily thanking Doctor Janki.

I was also felicitated by Unions and their leaders, one such leader said openly that Gokhale Saheb, your Net Work is definately stronger than ours. These words were much more meaningful than any appreciation.

Take Away :
- ➤ **How to behave calmly in difficult situations.**
- ➤ **In an emergency how to take systematic steps.**
- ➤ **Importance of TEAM WORK.**
- ➤ **How out of box thinking helps.**
- ➤ **How a social cause can also be a pedestal for marketing of Bank and creating a brand image.**
- ➤ **Have a magnanimous heart.**

• • •

(4) Unity in Diversity

Sitting in my cabin I was watching the transactions going on outside and at the same time conversing with the customers sitting across me. I was planning to visit my family residing at Pune, 500 Km. away on the forthcoming Saturday as Monday was a Public holiday. I had then communicated my plan to RM and obtained his oral approval to leave the headquarters.

I was observing that two Sisters from the orphanage were waiting for half an hour and were not comfortable. I went to them and enquired, what was the matter? One of them answered, 'We had deposited a cheque drawn on Calcutta office some 20 days back and the same was not yet credited. Your dealing officer informed us that the proceeds have been received yesterday only from Calcutta (Kolkata) and he will soon be releasing the concerned credit vouchers. We are waiting for credit in the account and even afterwards some more time would be required to collect cash from the cashier as our cheques are for more than Rs. 25,000/-, that is beyond the scope of the Teller.' They requested to look into the matter and help them. I gathered that the sisters belonged to the local branch of The 'Missionaries of Charity' an institution floated by Mother Teresa, a Nobel Laureate. However their office, school, the Orphanage they were running and the hospital were away from the city at a distance of around 30 Km. I arranged for quick disposal of their cash, passbook and cheque book

The Sisters came in my cabin and thanked me. They invited me to be present on Saturday evening at the orphanage to attend some function at their hospital. Their request was so heart felt that I agreed at once. Of course I had to reschedule my visit to Pune.

On Saturday I reached their office at around 4 pm. I was welcomed. Then came the 'Moment of truth.' The senior sister who welcomed me took me to the orphanage. My heart sank when I saw the pathetic conditions of the human suffering. Several of them were without fingers. Their wounds were lacerating with pus. Such was the serenity in air that I had to gather myself with courage. The condition of the patients and the smell in the air was so foul that I could not go beyond 3 to 4 feet. And the sisters were bandaging or applying some medicine to the wounds of the patients. I really felt ashamed of myself as they were serving the human beings where as I preferred to keep a distance from them.

The sisters informed that they were destitute. As they were suffering from some dreaded disease they were driven out from homes by their relatives. Some of them were in their terminal stages of life. Fortunately, I had brought some fruits. I handed over those and went back. But at that moment I resolved that I would do something for them.

On resuming my duties next working day I passed written instructions to the concerned department that the cheques of the Institution be immediately credited on the same day of receipt and only the actual courier charges be charged. Further I deliberately arranged a visit of all my staff members to the orphanage next Saturday and I swear the effect on them was very similar. I did not have to mention that after the visit to the institution there was a dramatic change in service yielded to the sisters. A suggestion came forward from one of the staff members which was supported by all that on various festive occasions such as New Year, Christmas, Diwali, Holi, Id, Independence day we would contribute and send some fruits to them. It was agreed and duly implemented.

On my own I used to purchase the seasonal fruits once a month and would send them to the hospital. On second or third visit to the wholesale market I met Mr. Sarfaraz, who recognized me and asked, 'Sir, why do you buy so many fruits? I know you are living alone and we are looking you here in Mandi for the 3rd time.' He was a wholesale merchant in fruits and used to receive funds from various places by T T (Telegraphic Transfer a mode of transmission of funds in vogue at that time). I used to allow payments to these vendors on case-to-case basis although there were some lacunae in the transmission of message. Most of them were Muslims. He persuaded me to tell the truth to whom I was giving the basketful of fruits. In a very humble way he told, 'Sir please give us also an occasion on this month of Ramzan to serve the human beings, otherwise Allah would nct like it!' He called his friends and told the story. They agreed and contributed a basket full of best lot of fruits every week. The practice continued not only during Ramzan but also in other months.

I must say that I am extremely thankful to our great Institution, Central Bank of India, that I was bestowed with a Branch Managership thereby I could contribute my mite to the society and of course to my parents and Mr. Periera, my colleague who had given me the practical lessons in serving human beings.

Take away :

> **Always sensitize your staff towards the customers. This has a tremendous impact on improvement in service.**

> **People should be given a chance to serve the society.**

> **Go beyond the rule book to help the people but always remember the interest of the Institution should be paramount!**

• • •

(5) Diwali

This was my second year of Diwali as a Branch Manager of Mumbai Main Office. We decided to celebrate it in a more dedicated way than what was done last year by contributing substantially from our own pockets. We decided to reach a target of at least 150 deserving mothers that is more than last year.

During last Diwali it was observed that there were plenty of clients who distributed sweets to all the staff members to celebrate Diwali. There were lots of sweets and particularly dry fruits distributed by various business / industrial houses. Initially I resisted accepting the same. But then I found that It was impossible to deny these things, as it was a tradition and considered as an exchange of well wishes. We found that, ultimately the dry fruits received during the Diwali reached to the tune of over 15 kgs. An idea struck in my mind that these things should go to the most deserving beneficiaries' i.e. the mothers of the new born or would be mothers, who are in real need of the proteins, carbohydrates, fats and vitamins. One of our lady colleagues came out with an idea that we should make small pouches of say 200 to 250 Gms. and then distribute them so that more mothers would be benefited. 'Sir, I take the responsibility to distribute the pouches with dry fruits in Madam Cama Hospital, where several mothers from the poor class are admitted'. One officer came forward and other lady officers along with two, three sub staff members took the initiative to prepare such pouches. Even a sub staff came on his own to supply sufficient pouches and also helped to distribute the same in the nearby Cama Hospital as his aunt was a Matron in the hospital. In no time 80 pouches were ready. One lady officer was so delighted that she contributed substantial money and ultimately a fund was collected so that we could prepare and gift 120 such pouches. This has definitely created awareness amongst staff to do and work for the well being of the society.

Considering our efforts, one of our clients M/S K R V Producer of Vitamins, added 150 bottles of Multi vitamin tablets to be given along with each pouch. We did receive the returns of our social commitment.

Take Away :

> ➤ **Thus we can celebrate various festivals in a true sense by remembering the needy people of the society.**

> ➤ **Our small but invaluable contribution would kindle a light of happiness and joy in their lives and in turn would give us an immense satisfaction.**

● ● ●

(6) Changing The Track

It was a month of October 1987 and I was posted in a village branch. The village had a population of about 2000. The other six nearby villages were attached to our branch. The villagers believed that Branch Managers are knowledgeable persons, who had answer to every question, they are capable to solve any problem.

In those days villagers often used to visit branches for the solutions from the Branch Managers as there were no other sources. Our village branch was not provided with a telephone connection. They needed consultation for various things. Such as: my pump set is not working what should I do? Which doctor should I consult? I want electric connection for my pump set, how shall I proceed? My son does not listen to me please advise him and what not? You will not believe, but one of my Brahmin manager colleague told that in a very interior village he had an occasion to act as a Pundit as the one who was to solemnize the marriage did not turn up. Of course the Manager had certain experience in the line as his father was a Pundit.

We were busy handling loan disbursements under the DRI Scheme. Shri Ramji Netam a cobbler by profession and also a DRI beneficiary was desirous to meet me. I could not help him as lots of applications were pending for disposal and we were surrounded by customers availing loan. Ultimately he entered the branch removing his chapples and stood up. But I could pay some attention to him only after 15 to 20 minutes. On asking him what the matter was, he simply kept quiet, I suggested him to come back at evening hours. Sahib, 'tomorrow morning,' he said and went away. He knew my arrival time and at 9 am generally no body used to be there. I communicated my assent.

When we were waiting for a bus my branch sub staff Shri Pramod informed me, 'Sir, perhaps Shri Ramji wants your help in case of his son.

Next morning when I reached the branch Shri Ramji was already present there. We exchanged welcome by Ram! Ram! I asked him to sit and offered a cup of tea. However he did not sit. I asked him,' what is the matter? Are you in need of some money?

Is somebody from your family not well? I was sure about money, as he had never defaulted in repayment of loan. He said no, by a gesture. Probably he was gathering the words to tell me his problem. Ultimately he came out and the sum and substance was,' His son Kamalakar, a Medical student and a bright boy, was not attending the college for last three months. Rather he joined the college in July and was very irregular right from the beginning. Shri Ramji wanted my help in this matter. He desired that I should advise him, so that he would continue to attend his classes. I assured him and told his son to come to the bank next day along with Kamalakar at around 2 pm. As it was non business day for the branch.

On the scheduled day I arrived at the branch at around 3pm after attending a morning meeting at Tehasil office. Mr Ramji was waiting along with his son Kamalakar. We as usual exchanged Ram! Ram! I patted Kamalakar as I knew him. We had felicitated him after his results. Our Head Cashier had left the branch to visit the nearby district branch to exchange soiled /torn currency notes. I was aware that the boy would not open up in the presence of others. After primary talks I told Shri Ramji to leave us alone.

It is an art to handle such cases, particularly the adolescent boys. I was fortunate that during my college days, I used to accompany Mrs. Laxmikaku, to a blind boy's school and hostel on Sundays and holidays. Mrs. Laxmikaku was a close friend of my mother. She was a Headmistress in a reputed school. She was also an expert Psychologist and and a rational human being. She taught me the art of storytelling and also how to handle the adolescents'. I always bow to her whenever I remember her!

I asked Kamlakar several questions about his college, his classmates, hostel life, the city he was living, playing Kabaddi (a game he was representing as a district player), latest movie he had seen, about his maternal uncle etc. Though I asked several questions I did give him sufficient time to speak and explain. For most of the time I was a keen and patient listener. All these questions were in fact **the Ice breakers.** Slowly I arrived at the point by seeking information about the various subjects, his professors and how he likes them?

Suddenly, he opened up, started sobbing; I patted him and took his hand in mine. And then he said slowly, 'I was telling my uncles that I am not interested to join Medical education. I did not like those subjects. I had then told them that I desire to join Engineering, but they did not listen. Sahib, you know that my parents are illiterate and my somewhat educated uncles forcibly admitted me to Medical College. I am unable to withstand the dissection, that smell of formalin and the visits to hospitals; rather I cannot digest these subjects. I would not intend to join Medical stream henceforth. Listening to this I came to the conclusion that his non-acceptance was in fact a Phobia for the medical course.

Then, I changed the track and asked him some friendly casual questions about his local friends. I ordered some hot snacks and tea. We then resumed, he clearly was having tilt towards engineering education. He told confidently that if given a chance to learn engineering stream, he will not only regularly attend the college but will put all efforts as he had done in 12th standard. He had a nice score of over 88% but missed the merit by a whisker. I assured him that I would speak with others and then we will keep meeting. He left with an assured smile.

Now the ball was in my court and I had a task to convince his parents and uncles.

I discussed the pros and cons with one of the most learned and respected person of the village, Kakaji Deshpande. He was a scholar of Sanskrit and a philanthropist. He had donated 10 acres of his road side fertile land and contributed substantial amount for school building. Two of his sons were Wing Commanders in Indian Air Force. The elder son was subsequently promoted as Air Vice Marshal. The youngest was a reputed Advocate. His daughter was a senior scientist with ISRO. Kakaji was a person Ideal, respected and loved by the villagers belonging to all caste and creed. He used to help every needy person in the village. Similar was his wife solving the difficulties of the women creed. If there was any dispute between the relatives, or between persons, they would approach Kakaji who had an uncanny knack to resolve the problems. I have never met such a generous wife and husband in my life. They were very similar to my parents. They used to love me as a son. Kakaji also supported my view that the student be helped to Change the Track from Medical to Engineering. He gave me the parental advice to speak with the Headmaster of the school. We then called his parents and relatives, the head master and Kamlakar to resolve the issue. 'Though I will be present, you have to take the lead, he told. Headmaster on meeting clarified that at the first hand only he had opined that Kamalakar should join engineering and not what his uncles wanted.

I then called the meeting of all concerned. We invited the Sarpanch of the village. Of course, I had briefed him and he was also of the opinion to support the side of the student.

The meeting held on the auspicious day of Sri Ramnvami. The venue of the meeting was, of course the residence of Shri Kakaji. I elaborately explained the situation. At first there was resistance from uncles of Kamalakar, but Kamlakar was firm on his decision. Consequently the uncles yielded but with a condition that he should get admission in the Engineering College. Thus through great perseverance, guidance and advice of elders one hurdle was surpassed. Earlier Shri Ramji father of Kamlaker had told me, 'Sahib please do the best thing for my son.' He also happily gave consent to the change of Kamlakar`s track.

Our sub staff Mr. Praomod, who knew the entire case said, 'Sir you have tackled the entire situation nicely and special thanks from my younger brother who is the close friend of Kamalakar. Sir, may I suggest you?' I consented. He gave me vital information, 'Sir recently Shri Deshmukh had joined the University as The Registrar, he belonged to our village. You should meet him. He is a nice person.'

Next day, I had to visit RO for certain work. I decided to take a chance, since the University and RO were at the same district place. I fixed an appointment with Shri Deshmukh. He was very happy to receive me since I was from his village. He was extremely happy to listen to the entire episode about Kamalaker.

He also appreciated my initiative taken for the son of the soil. He assured to support Kamalakar and gave me a letter favouring The Principal of The Engineering College. Then it was a cake walk for me. The Principal was very co-operative. He straight away arranged application form for admission in the second semester which was beginning from December. In those days the admissions for Engineering or Medical Colleges were merely based on the score of 12th standard.

Later on I came to know that presently Mr. Kamalakar is a Senior Engineer in L and T. He is the HNW Customer of our Village Branch and does not fail to ask about my where about. The World is round and perhaps we may meet again. My Best wishes to him.

Take Away :

➢ **Almighty always helps those who keep on trying!**

➢ **Listening is an art one must develop.**

➢ **For solving any problem one has to take view from all angles.**

● ● ●

(7) Corporate Social Responsibility

It was a Sunday and I was leisurely reading a news paper. Around 11am, Mr. Damodar, the Branch Manager of Rajkot branch called on me at my residence along with an unknown person. We exchanged 'Namaste'. Mr. Damodar said, 'Sir, I am visiting you on Sunday without appointment, but I know that you generally keep this time of Sundays reserved for Inspection of new units and I took a chance since matter was important. Sir, here is Shri Sumitbhai. He is the partner of M/S Ganesh Orthopedic Products.' We shook hands. Then Mr. Damodar informed me that, the unit has a gala in Pratap Industrial Estate and they are shifting their unit from Mumbai. Yesterday there was a social function at Shri Ramanbhai's residence, our neighbour. Incidentally we, Shri Sumitbhai and myself were common guests. During the discussion I came to know that their present banker is Syndicate Bank, Mumbai and they are enjoying only working capital limits of Rs 30 lakhs. They had fixed an appointment with local Syndicate Bank on Tuesday in respect of the proposed unit. I may add that our neighbour who is also a distant relative of Shri Sumitbhai had appreciated his business acumen. I had no point to say no and hence we proceeded towards the Pratap Industrial Estate. On way Mr. Sumeetbhai informed us that they are in the business of manufacturing the Ortho Solutions for last 5 years and doing fairly well.

On reaching the unit, we found that a small shed was already built and one lathe machine, one CNC machine and others were already on the shop floor. The construction work of the shed was in progress. He explained that these Machines were transported from their Mumbai Unit.

On seeking reasons for shifting, he gave the following explanation: The present area of the unit at Mumbai was to be handed over to the Corporation, since a ring road was being built. We had been offered an alternate place to shift. But the allotted place has no space for expansion. The labourers were also reluctant to join new place. A dumping ground was very close and hence the allotted area was not hygienic and suitable. We had purchased this plot in Pratap Industrial Estate five years back. Our skilled labourers are from UP and hence they had no issue once housing is provided to them.' The reasons put forth were convincing.

On going through the financial results, the turnover of the firm was found to be around Rs 5 Crores. On a cursory look the other financial ratios were also found satisfactory. They were holding the requisite licenses. The power sanction was on hand. The statement of Cash Credit account at Syndicate Bank was reflecting satisfactory operations.

We then asked about their production plan, range of finished products, marketing plan and their credit requirements.

We sought the detailed plan about the proposed building containing production area, administration blocks, storage space for raw materials and finished goods and block for research and development. They were also requested to furnish the details of necessary electrical cabling, fixtures, transformer, AC units, other machinery and furniture and fixtures.

Shri Sumitbhai informed, that the product range encompasses orthopedic and traumatological implants and instruments and vertebral products. They would provide to the patients with plates for mini, small and large fragments, DHS and DCS plates, cortical screws and various other screws. We manufacture these products in a variety of versions from carefully-selected raw materials.

On asking him about what would be the raw materials. He replied, 'there would be two types of finished products, one will be products with low range of costs which will be made from High-alloyed steel, and second type of finished products will be high range products which would be manufactured from pure Titanium or alloyed Titanium.'

'For this project, apart from two lathe machines we will require three CNC machines, computers with modern CAD/CAM systems. We propose to manufacture standard products, prototype products as well as tailor made products,' argued Shri Sumitbhai.

'We have already developed chain of distributors of our products in Gujrat, Maharashtra, Tamilnadu and Madhya Pradesh. Recently we have established good links with Apollo hospital and hospitals in all metro cities. Soon we will have our distributors in all 1'st class cities like Bangalore, Hyderabad, Nagpur, Raipur, Kanpur, Allahabad, Jaipur. In Dubai my brother is looking after the sales,' added Shri Sumitbhai.

Shri Sumitbhai further made it clear that credit facilities required would include Term Loan, Foreign Currency Loan and of course Working Capital as well as Letter of Credit and Bank Guarantee. We are working on exact requirement and Project Report will be ready in a day or two.

The overall project was convincing. As a result I told Shri Sumitbhai then and there only that, 'We have in Principle Approval.' He was looking at us with a surprise, for such a quick decision! Within a fortnight a regular Credit Proposal was put forth through the branch to RO and on the basis of appraisal suitable credit facilities were sanctioned.

We again visited the Industrial unit before the disbursement. We were introduced to the senior partner, Shri Narayanbhai, father of Shri Sumitbhai. He was pleased with the speed with which the proposal was sanctioned and also the disbursement stage was reached. After light refreshment and a cup of tea I told Shri Narayanbhai, 'I have one demand and stopped speaking!' Listening this Shri Narayanbhai, Shri Sumitbhai as also Mr. Damodar our Branch Manager were baffled. I deliberately kept silence. The pressures was building, but then breaking the silence Shri Narayanbhai said meekly, please tell us. I then further asked that they should give assurance in advance. Shri Narayanbhai understood that now there was no alternative,and hence gave concurrence by saying 'OK' in a low voice. I deliberately took some time and then spoke, 'since you have assured I thank you at the first hand and I desire that, you will donate every year at least five such kits to the most needed.'

Now the entire group present went into a pin drop silence. And then Shri Narayanbhai smiled happily and his face was glittering with joy. He stood at once and took my hand with great warmth. He reflected, 'Sahib, why only five units? We will donate at least 10 such kits.'

I further added that I had already met HoD of Orthopaedic Department of Government Medical College and he had agreed to pass on the details of the needy patients. The son of one of our staff members, was a Doctor in the Government Medical College. Through him I contacted the HoD. Now Mr. Damodar, my Branch Manager was looking at me proudly!

We further suggested several additions to the project, to be implemented in stages:

1. Introducing full AC facilities in the manufacturing area.
2. Using gloves to reduce any human intervention.
3. Dress code to all.
4. Invariably changing dress before going inside the Manufacturing area.

5. All input material should meet strict quality standards in consonance with the international norms.
6. Electro polishing, manual polishing, sand blasting and careful final inspection be undertaken before packing.
7. Proper and intelligent warehouse storage.
8. Technical staff be given continuous advanced training and education.

All these factors would ensure that the products meet the highest levels of standard.

I had an occasion to speak with the Branch Manager of the concerned branch (Mar 2015). He was extremely happy with the dealings of the said client. They had crossed the sales of Rs18 crores. He told that Shri Narayanbhai always talks very high about me. They have implemented all our suggestions.

The Company not only helps 10 poor patients but now has a separate CSR Department to handle the yeomen activity.

Take Away :

➤ **Always look out for opportunities to develop business.**

➤ **Sensitize your staff and also help them to develop this skill.**

➤ **Decision making is a function of information, removing the grain from the chaff and intuition.**

➤ **Kindle the lamp in your customers to contribute for the society.**

➤ **Always advise the customer to develop the Best Practices in every sphere.**

● ● ●

Products of the Firm : Implants to Support Bones

● ● ●

(8) How Are You Concerned?

It was the end of the rainy season; however the disbursement of the final instalment of Agriculture loan was going on. We were having a sizeable number of accounts and last few days were very busy days. Looking outside my cabin I was observing that Shri Lingappa, an agriculturist was sitting on the bench right from 10, O'clock and it was already 4 pm. I called him but he stayed on till the last person from his village went away. It was almost 6 pm when he came in. I asked him about his sugar cane crop. I knew that his crop was one of the best though his land holding was only around 6 acres. On this question he immediately opened up and told me about the conditions of the crop, the Agri operations he had undertaken etc. Then he stopped speaking, perhaps gathering the words to tell the story.

He began, 'Sir, my son Ramlu who is in the 8th standard is studying in Modern School in Latur city. This school is one of the famous schools in the entire State for having very high standards of education. Every year the Merit list would include at least 4 to 5 students from this school and 100 % result was another credit. The admission to the school was tough and it was but obvious that the student once admitted will have a bright career. Ramlu got admitted in Modern School this year after completing 7th standard from the village school. Ramlu was a very bright student throughout his career in his village school. He had come back from the school after 15th August and not resuming. I took him twice to the school but somehow he returned from Latur. His class teacher was also complaining about his inattentiveness. Sir, please help me.'

I advised him to come to the branch along with Ramlu at about 3 pm on the next Saturday.

Next working day I called Mrs. Varsha Naik, one of our staff, a mother of two school going children, an efficient worker and a very rational lady and discussed with her about Ramlu. She had a background of child Psychology, a subject of her liking in her college career as informed by her during a birth day party. We had decided a course to be followed the day on which Ramlu and his father was called.

On Saturday as scheduled both of them were present at around 3 pm, I called them in my cabin and asked them to sit. As decided earlier Mrs.Varsha came in seeking some information and reminding me about the scheduled meeting at 3.30 pm. She and Lingappa exchanged 'Namaste.' She smiled at the child and patted him. She casually questioned Lingappa, 'your son? Very bright child'. Shri Lingappa introduced Ramlu to her. Then she told Shri Lingappa that Mr Ashok our Loan department in charge is calling you for some work please go and meet him. I also went away for the meeting. Now on Mrs. Varsha and Ramlu were inside. She took out some candy and gave it to Ramlu. I left the office as decided and came back at around 5 pm to find no body except the guard. We closed the branch and I returned to my residence.

Next morning I got a telephone call from Mr. Naik, incidentally a banker to join for the breakfast. Of course I happily accepted the invitation as I was alone. While enjoying our breakfast Mrs. Varsha narrated the interaction with Ramlu in a very lively manner. The sum and substance was, Ramlu was from a very small village, he had his education in Marathi medium, he could not converse in English like others, his hostel colleagues used to laugh at him. He felt very odd and unable to face them and hence he was not attending the school. She further told me that she was able to convince Ramlu to rejoin the school. He agreed only when she assured him that his school teachers will support him in learning all the subjects in English.

Our breakfast ended with a question by Mr. Naik. He asked 'Of all the things I could not understand one thing and that was, **How are you concerned?'** The question I had to face umpteen times in future conversations. I just smiled and left after thanking the couple.

On Monday I telephoned my Branch Manager colleague at Latur to find, the telephone number of the school. His query was, 'Gokhaleji, I know that your son and daughter are already graduates, then why do you need 'this information required by you.' I told the entire story of Ramlu he said 'I understood, but **How are you concerned?'** I just thanked him, smiled and put the receiver down.

After obtaining the telephone number of the school, I rang up the Head Master, introduced myself and then requested him to help Ramlu. When I spoke about Ramlu, he immediately asked, 'Are you speaking about the boy who was not attending the school for last two months?' 'Yes', I answered and also explained my relations as a banker with the father of the student. In an astonishing tone he said, I See! I told him about the support Ramlu wanted. He agreed to pay the personal attention but advised to speak with the Class teacher. He said 'ok!' But may I ask you a question 'and again came the question, but Mr. Gokhale, **How are you concerned?'**

He then called the class teacher Mr. Deshmukh; in a nut shell I repeated the entire story. He was aware of the shortcoming of Ramlu and assured that he will give him an early morning special tuition. He said further I am impressed that you are taking the personal interest in the education of a child. But may I ask you a question? **'How are you concerned?'** I ended our conversation with a smile after thanking him. I was keeping the track of Ramlu for the next two years. Then I was transferred and resumed the new branch. One day I received a call from Mrs. Varsha. Her voice was very excited, she informed, 'Sir our Ramlu stood in the Merit list for SSC! I congratulated her adding, 'but for your efforts, otherwise a student would have lost his future!'

I had no track of Ramlu from then onwards, but I wish he must be doing very well in his field! My best wishes to him.

Take Away :
- Interest of a customer is the interest of a banker.
- Understand the skills your staff possess, recognize them, help them to apply and derive a satisfaction out of them.
- Always invest some time for a social cause, the returns will be bountiful!

• • •

Sow a thought, reap an action; Sow an action reap a habit ; Sow a habit reap a character;Sow a character reap a destiny.— Samuel Smiles

6 | DIFFICULT SITUATIONS FACED DURING BANKING CAREER

(1) Fire in the Safe Deposit Vault

There was a loud thud from the basement of the branch and thick smoke clouds started spreading everywhere. We ran downstairs by the staircase towards the basement from where the smoke was emanating.

Those were the days of monsoon in Mumbai and at that time of the year it was really raining cats and dogs. Our bank would be celebrating the Centenary year soon and hence Mumbai Main Branch, the earlier Head Office of the bank was under renovation. The prestigious *'Monumental Heritage Building' of the Bank comprising of 7 floors and the two basements* was under renovation. While the outside façade was to be kept untouched as per Heritage Act, the inside was going under repairs and total facelift. The area of each floor was more than 8400 Sq. feet. One time The Mumbai Main Office (MMO) in 1980's was the biggest branch in Asia and around 2000 personnel were working in that building. The different groups handling different activities such as POP, Masonry, Carpentry, Electrical, Data cable fixing, AC plant operations, Lift repairing, Painting, Glass fitting, Telephone cabling, Welding, Casual labourers were working together to complete the work before the proposed date. Rains were very heavy and the building was not repaired earlier causing lot of seepages at many places. Fixing this major problem was also being undertaken. There was a room given for transformer and other electrical fittings to MSEB (an electricity board) in the basement near the Safe Deposit Vault and there was seepage from some cable from 7th floor. Perhaps this had caused the short circuit in that Electrical room and hence the loud thud and smoke was literally oozing out in the Safe Deposit Vault and upstairs. Earlier before running downstairs I had called our security officer to urgently summon the Main electrician who was well aware about the electrical cabling plan and two other staff to get 3 to 4 fire extinguishers for electric fire. Fortunately the Electrician listening the sound also came down in seconds and removed the relevant fuses thereby cutting the power supply. In the mean time our Security officer successfully extinguished the fire, however smoke was still coming out of the cable and room. It was pitch dark and very smokey right from the huge entrance door of the vault, when we reached there. Somehow our vault officer had produced a torch and we had mobile torches. Vault officer informed that he had pulled out two lady customers, but two aged customers were still inside. There are about 5000 lockers in the locker room. We immediately tied wet napkins on our mouth, two of us went in. It was not only absolute dark but also full of smoke inside. The customers were making some sound and somehow we literally pulled them out and took them upstairs. They were reluctant to come up as their vault was open and the belongings were on table. We assured them about their valuables, served them with some water and cold drinks. Now the smoke had also subsided and our electrician successfully detached and cut off the faulty cable, restored the power supply. I left The Safe Deposit customers in the hands of my efficient PA. Then again I ran downstairs where my Security officer and other staff were near the entrance guarding the vault. Inside it was still very smokey. The entire room being very similar to a steel ship with windows and hence smoke was not dispersing. We then fixed some huge stand fans to drive smoke out, still the entire operation took about 2 hours.

Then we searched all the cabins with a pounding heart and

had a sigh of relief to find that they were all empty! Next we took our two senior customers downstairs along with two other customers and two officers to their relevant open lockers. The customers were requested to take inventory in presence of the other two persons. They were satisfied with their belongings and thanked us. I apologized as we had then dealt with them a bit sternly. But now they were smiling with satisfaction. In the mean time my PA as directed, brought two letters of satisfaction and they were duly signed by the said customers and countersigned by two others as witness.

I specially called the meeting of all the staff members and appreciated the concerned staff from the vault, security personnel and the electrician for their timely action. Not only this but also on the eve of opening Ceremony of The Renovated MMO Branch as a part of **A Centenary Function of The Bank** all the concerned were felicitated through the hands of our Chairman and Managing Director.

Take Away :

➢ **Remember a person is tested for his qualities in emergency.**

➢ **The best style of leadership under such conditions is Dictatorial style.**

➢ **Leader himself should keep calm and composed.**

➢ **Observe that fire gadgets be always maintained and the drill be also followed at least once in a year.**

➢ **Remember to create a record of things, as confirmation, witness etc.**

➢ **Never miss any chance to recognize the staff at the same instant and felicitate them through higher authorities!**

• • •

(2) Remittance on a Monson Day

The Monsoon was in the middle and at its full fury. Particularly during last two days there were very heavy rains. Today it was quite all right since morning and therefore I agreed to the suggestion of my Head Cashier to remit Cash to the nearest designated branch which was at a distance of about 30 Km. from our village branch. The other reason was our holding was much more than the threshold limit. Our cash safe was literally full and did not have any capacity to hold further cash. There were holidays on the next two days and in such case excess holding of cash was fraught with risk. The receiving branch was agreeable to receive cash even after normal timings; this was also confirmed by the receiving branch over telephone from the local sub Post Office.

Our branch was close to the road and located in between the two Tehasil places. Those were the days (1985) when communication facilities were not developed. There were only two telephones in the village one at Sub Post Office and the other at one of the merchants. Our village branch was not provided with a telephone. The one and only available means of communication was State Transport buses and those too had only three schedules in a day. As per the system followed for remittance our Head Cashier accompanied with one sub staff and with a Cash Box boarded the State Transport bus at around 11.30 am so as to reach the designated branch at about 12.30 pm. Again at around 12.30 pm it started raining heavily. It was expected that Head Cashier after reaching there would telephone to the Post Master who used to communicate us. However on the fateful day there was no confirmation telephone up to 3 pm. On enquiring we learnt that the telephone was dead, a common phenomenon on a rainy day. Also there was no traffic on the road and the scheduled buses travelling on either side had not crossed at our village branch at their usual timing of 3.30 pm. We were waiting and waiting for some response from the receiver branch end or from our HC but we received none till 6 pm. We were worried but we could do little since there was absolutely no traffic from either side nor the telephone links. It was getting dark and heavy rains had begun again. Our staff was carrying a Cash of over Rs. 3 lakhs which was a huge sum at that time (Gold was Rs1500 for 10 gms). The worried relatives of the staff members also called on us as they were aware that the concerned staff had gone to the nearest Tehasil branch for banks' work. We tried for a motorcycle but because of incessant rains we had to drop that idea. However at around 6.30 pm we received a call from the Tehasil branch that buses from our village had not reached and our cashier had not reported their branch. Now it was clear that they were stuck up somewhere in between the two culverts and there was no way reaching them. The villagers told that it must be in between the village named Pimplod which had two culverts on both sides and due to heavy rains they must be overflowing.

I was really worried as they had cash and it was very risky to keep it safely in a ST Bus. Some other way had to be thought, so I went to the Post Office again which was our only means of communication. We tried to call the Sub Post Office at Pimplod but the land lines were snapped and hence the contact could not be established. We had to think some other way and it struck to me, that I could take the help of police? On discussion with the Post Master on this issue, he told me that, Shri Deshmukh from our village was in wireless department in police at Tehasil place Akot which was falling on the other side of our branch. We put up a call to police at Akot and with great difficulty could speak with Mr. Deshmukh. Incidentaly he was knowing me and agreed to help me immediately. We requested him to know through the wireless whether our Head Cashier was in Pimplod and whether he was safe and if possible could he communicate with Shri Deshmukh through Police wireless. After half an hour we received a call from Shri Deshmukh that our Cashier reached Pimplod at about 12.30 pm and stranded there in the State Transport bus as on both ends of the road the culverts were overflowing, but he was safe with cash. Then I communicated back to him to speak with Shri Guhe, Branch Manager of a Cooperative Bank at Pimplod who was from our village and may be stranded in their branch and requested him to exchange cash for the Demand Draft. The entire conversation was going on through wireless with the help of Police. Still I was worried about the safety of my staff, as it was already 9 pm.

Now after doing my part of the job, nothing was in our control but to wait and watch. We were praying to the Rain Gods, be merciful and give some respite. I decided to stay at the branch premises which were on the road side with the hope that if rain stopped my staff members would return to the branch. It was pitch dark and still raining heavily. The branch was at a bit secluded place, away from the village. I still shiver when I remember how I passed that night in a pitch dark condition, pouring rains; the frogs, the cricket and various other insects making strange fearful sounds and the moaning of the dogs. Worried but equally exhausted I was dozing but fell asleep, when I do not know.

I was aroused by our cashier at around 7 am next morning. He was surprised to find me waiting for him. My cashier was all praise for Shri Guhe, the Branch Manager of Cooperative Bank, that he had received the cash, issued a Demand Draft on its district branch and that too at about 10 pm and also helped them to be comfortable

The drama ended after about 20 hours of the excruciating waiting and worrying period but with a satisfaction that my people and all important asset of the bank i.e. the cash was guarded safely at Pimplod.

During the next Branch Anniversary Programme we felicitated Mr.Deshmukh from Police, Mr Guhe Branch Manager of the Cooperative Bank and local Post Master for their help. I also arranged to send an Appreciation Letters through our Regional Manager to the concerned, District Police Headquarters and to the Head Office of the Cooperative Bank and of course to my brave sub staff and the Head Cashier.

Take Away :

➢ **In difficult situations think of all possible solutions.**

> Establish a network of reliable people on whom you can rely at difficult times.
> Face all difficult situations with self confidence and courage.
> Never forget to recognize the people who had helped you and your staff.

• • •

(3) The Black Cat

My parents belonged to a very typical Hindu clan. Both were very religious, ardently following the rules and regulations which were usually followed in the contemporary Hindu family, but they were very rational while dealing with human beings'. They had a magnanimous heart and would not mind helping others to the last penny in their pocket. I did borrow a miniscule of their goodness. I have a religious bent of mind, a great liking for the people and of course a rational thinking.

On that fateful day, we me and my colleague Mr. Swamy were just crossing the road from our building to catch an auto rickshaw to reach the railway station and thence to office. At that time Mr. Swamy literally dragged me three steps backward as **'a black cat',** a pet of our neighbour was crossing the road. I was absolutely not a believer in such superstitions and forgot the incident before I reached the office at about 10 am. As usual, I was busy attending my work when at around 11.30 am me and my senior manager were summoned by a Senior Executive. When we reached in the cabin we were taken right and left for our certain decision. The fury of the questions from the person was so bombastic that we were nonplussed and were only listening for half an hour without opening our mouth. The way and words used to hit us were unusually harsh. We were then asked about the decision, whether it was wrong or right? When we tried to explain that it was as per our rule book, the person retorted that throw it in the dust bin. On our further explanation that we had put up the matter to our immediate boss and obtained his concurrence, the concerned was furious with him also. Another senior officer was called and he was told to issue a suspension orders to two of us. We were asked to receive the same. We were out and soon the news spread in our department. Our department personnel were astonished as they knew the case. It was Saturday and we did receive a Suspension orders from our boss, although he was not in agreement with this action and even tried to advocate our side. We were perturbed but remained calm and composed without making any unreasonable action. However before leaving, I informed to my immediate higher authority that we had to conduct examination for recruitment next Sunday and he had to make urgent alternative arrangement as I was the conductor of those examinations. He showed his regret and inability to do anything but requested us to attend the office on Monday. We were called by another Executive, who knew us for over 15 years, patiently heard all that happened and told us to remain calm; he also assured us that he will try to intervene in the matter. We left the office at around 3 pm. I boarded a train and left to join my family living in the nearby city, worried I was but not knowing for what!

I spent Sunday with my family in a gloomy set of mind, though my wife never questioned me about my mood, I was sure that she must have understood that something unusual had happened with me. I was not my usual self, never the less she very silently and without words did show her full support to me and I cannot explain in words how soothing it was.

Next day early morning, I left as I used to do on Mondays. We were called again by the same Executive who had earlier flossed us. The person asked us whether we were ready to accept transfer to North East instead of suspension. We remained quiet, showing our non acceptance. The reaction was perhaps due to intervention by our friendly Executive. We went out. The news of our suspension spread throughout the office and staff across all unions started gathering at the entrance, the ladies staff was particularly very vociferous. I was urgently called by our friendly Executive and he advised me not to precipitate the matter. I told him that I did not make any such move but it was a voluntary reaction on the part of the staff. I had to intervene and request the Union Leaders not to make such a move. Then only the mob dispersed but they warned that they may redo the act for showing the solidarity towards us. Our friend again met and perhaps explained the situation to the angry Executive. The day passed like that creating tension.

Next morning, we were again summoned and the officer who had served the suspension order was also called and of course our friendly Executive was also present there. Then the concerned Executive warned us not to take such decisions and furiously questioned our boss why he had served the suspension orders and thundered that those should be torn and thrown into dust bin now and here.

The action of suspension was thus reversed and all the records were also removed.

Afterwards I understood that the root cause of that forgettable episode was a severe shortage of the expert staff. This had severely affected the completion of the vital projects as planned. As a result, the concerned Executive had to look down before the public and face a fury of Government Officials for non compliance. But it was also true that we were the unfortunate scapegoats!

The reason for the entire episode was, two lady members were appointed as specialist officers. Immediately after joining, they were deputed for one month training. On completing the training they applied for leave initially for a period of 3 months on medical grounds. The leave application along with the certificate from the bank's panel doctor was forwarded to our department for sanction as per rules. The leave was sanctioned by me and the concerned lady officers were communicated that their leave would be treated as sanctioned leave on loss of pay and their confirmation period would also be extended further by the even period as per applicable standing rules. Further, we had put up a note on this to our immediate higher authorities and he had signed the approval of our action. On this issue our department had taken all the necessary steps and acted exactly as per rule book.

On that very eventful day of happening me and my colleague Mr. Swamy returned home at about 8 pm and found that my neighbours with his family members were mourning the accidental death of their pet **Black Cat**. We also joined them.

What a co-incidence?

Take Away :

➢ **Remember that all days in your work life will never be the same. There would be the days of frustration but never lose the peace of mind; face it and remain calm.**

➢ **Create a record of what you have done. It always speaks the truth.**

➢ **Always keep the interest of your Institution as prime and never fail in your duties, whatever may be the circumstances.**

➢ **In an official capacity whenever you are criticized or bashed by your Boss or Customers never take it personally, but remember it is always directed towards the chair you adore.**

➢ **Create your value whereever you are working, so that people will be on your side in difficult circumstances.**

➢ **Always be up-right, as Truth is eternal.**

• • •

(4) The Joining Day

After getting promotion, I was very happy on the joining day of my new assignment as I was the first and only Senior Manager in the Region and that too posted in a prestigious Bajaj Factory branch. In past, Regional Manager and me had worked in one of the branches. As such he knew me very well and hence I was welcomed by him in a fabulous way. He not only arranged a small welcome function but also arranged his vehicle for reaching me to the proposed prestigious branch along with one of his staff members, a very rare gesture in the banking industry. It took 45 minutes to reach us the branch. It was at a distance of about 25 Kms. from the city. I took charge of the branch and got acquainted with the staff. Since I was a faculty member in my earlier assignment most of the staff knew me.

The staff was cooperative and they quickly gave me the feedback. The main client was of course Bajaj Auto. There were not many savings or fixed deposit accounts as it was purely an Industrial Area. There were two critical accounts and the concerned credit officer explained me that they need a close monitoring. My accountant was persuing me to go for the factory visit and I decided to have a firsthand feel of one of the Units on the very day as the Unit was very close to the branch. We did visit the plant and on a cursory look it was clear that some of the machines were not working, there was an excessive finished goods stock and substantial rejected stock. On going through accounts there were huge amount of devolved LC's. Cash credit and Overdraft accounts were slightly overdrawn and the Bills purchased account was also showing the history of returned bills. The overall health of the account was not well.

We returned with this feel of the account and then took the lunch along with all the staff. I made it clear to the staff that my posting in this branch was for completing the rural stint of four months but I would work as a permanent Branch Manager and requested them to contribute for the development of the business. The staff was now closing their work as it was around 3.30 pm and the working hours were up to 4 pm. The staff was briefing me about the working of Computer system as this was my first exposure to new technology and the branch was one of the few branches in India with partial computerization (it was way back in 1999).

A telephone rang and one of my colleagues told me that Regional Manager would like to speak with me; I went in my cabin and with a little surprise and attended the phone call. After the exchange of the usual pleasantry he told me that a proposal for a temporary overdraft for about Rs. 45 lakhs from the Unit which I had visited was pending for last few days at the branch. The Unit was in dire need of the funds and the sum was to be disbursed for issuance of Demand Drafts today only. I listened to him and stated that since I had joined on that day I did not have a clear picture of the working of the Unit and would need some time to judge. He told me that the MD of the Unit was sitting in my office and it was absolutely necessary to disburse the funds today. He added that, 'We knew each other very well and you are always a knowledgeable, pragmatic person. You can understand the urgency of an Industrial Unit'. He was persuing me to go ahead and that too urgently as next two days were holidays.

In fact I was not aware of and sure about the end use of the funds. Besides the credit limits were sanctioned by The Zonal Office. To extend such a loan was beyond my discretionary / sanctioning powers. Now I understood why all that welcome was extended to me.

I told him that it would be really difficult to follow the request and if he would give his concurrence I would arrange the DD's. Credit officer was silently listening on the parallel telephone as directed by me and he shown his assent by a gesture. RM was little perturbed. He told me in a different tone that it was a time of closure of the branch and how he could furnish the sanction and how DD's could be issued as it was already 4 pm. But I communicated that I would arrange everything as assented by my colleague over the parallel phone by way of a hand and head gesture. Now my RM was bit disturbed, he ordered me to go ahead and said the proposal may be sent to him afterwards and he would sanction it. But there was no confidence in his tone. I informed him that the proposal would be on his table in about an hour and I would manage the entire show today only.

In fact the proposal was ready two days before my joining but not recommended as no Branch Manager was posted. I just added that since the undersigned had no occasion to go through the detailed factual position of the unit the proposal was put forth for your consideration on merits. I had not added my recommendations. I deputed credit officer to RO to communicate the orders of the sanction by fax. My other officer colleague suggested to keep the DD's ready and hand over to the client only after receiving the sanction. I gave my assent and the DD's were ready by 6 pm.

We were ready and as expected I received a call from RM, he was a bit furious but I cleared my position that without full knowledge it would be difficult for me to add my recommendations.

We received the sanction through our officer waiting at RO by a fax. The DD's were handed over to the MD at about 7 pm and we closed down. In a way it was a win -win position for me and Regional Manager.

The account slipped to NPA during the next financial year and Regional Manager had to face the music.

Take Away :

> **Take decisions only after receiving full information of all related aspects.**
> **Listen to the feedback from your colleagues.**
> **Learn to say No with a sugarcoating.**

• • •

(5) The Court Case

I was far away from the place of posting enjoying leave travel facility at Kashmir. I was purturbed when I received a telephone call from our Banks' Advocate informing me that my presence is required in one of the important court cases and the case was on board for hearing after 4-5 days. I was a bit worried as till that date I had no occasion to appear before a Judge. Similarly, there was no clarity about the case.

The bank had filed a case against the proprietorship concern M/S ABC as there were no satisfactory operations and account was overdrawn than available Drawing Power (DP) as there was absolutely very low stock. The client had issued several cheques but they were returned as DP was not available. The bank had classified the account as bad and doubtful (i.e. Non Performing

Asset in today's context). The bank had attached the factory and taken possession of whatever inventory that was available. This was done in presence of the court Commissioner. A statement of the detailed stock taken in possession was prepared in the presence of the borrower and duly signed by all including me on the day.

M/S ABC had filed the counter case demanding compensation of a huge amount in damages as his factory as well the inventory was attached. He had pleaded that there was sufficient inventory and hence DP was available to honour all the 12-15 cheques which were dishonored by the bank during last few months. This had caused a great damage to his reputation and closure of his business and hence huge losses for which the bank was responsible. For supporting his plea he had filed 2 Statements of Stock (Inventory) and Debtors for the months of June and July, indicating availability of huge stocks and hence sufficient DP, so he pleaded about the wrongful dishonor of cheques. He claimed a compensation of over Rs 1crore, a very huge sum at that time (1985). In the said statements of Inventory and Debtors produced by him for 2 months, contained the verification purported to be signed by me. Based on these documents he had claimed the compensation from the bank. On this issue our advocate wanted my presence in the court.

On reaching the place of posting, I called on our advocate. He showed me the Xerox copies of those verified statements. I was literally dumb folded looking at them. I did tell him the signatures were apparently of mine but it was not our practice to write verification remarks on such stock statements. I told him that I did not remember having put any such remarks. But all these things had created a lot of flutter not only in my mind but also in the minds of our Branch Manager. Our Advocate Shri Sule was quite composed as he was one of the most reputed and intelligent lawyer in the town. He told us not to be perturbed and asked us to collect all the stock statements for the past one year, financial statements for last two years as well as the Income Tax and Sales Tax Statements.

On the day of appearance I was shown the said statements and our lawyer asked me several questions about the veracity of them. He recorded that the said statements were the photocopies and requested the court to give some more time as he had to produce some more documents as evidence. An adjournment of seven days was given. I left the court with a pounding heart and would suffer the same for another seven days.

Before the next date we collected all the relevant documents and handed over the same to Advocate Sule. On the proposed day, I sworn in and he got all the said documents along with the stock statements verified by me. The various dates of receipt endorsed were also verified. He completed his examination in chief and then began the cross examination by the defense advocate. He asked me several searching questions, but I was very straight and only answered that the two stock statements under question for the months of June and July, were the Xerox copies and there was no system to endorse such statements and I did not remember having put such remarks at any time on those statements though the signatures were apparently mine.

Then the examination in Chief of the proprietor of M/S ABC was carried out followed by the cross examination by our advocate. Again all the above said statements were shown to the defense for his perusal, he agreed on it. Then statement of account was shown to him by our advocate. The defense deposed that bank had not extended the funds during the period from Jan to June. Our advocate produced some letters given to the bank by the defendant that he had no money to purchase Raw material and he was not getting the credit from the market during the period. Also the Tax returns, Balance Sheet, Profit and loss account, purchase account reflecting no capacity to bring in the stock were presented to the court. The sum and substance was proving that he had no avenue to bring in the fresh stock for that huge amount during the months of June and July. While closing the arguments our advocate propounded that those two monthly statements were only Xerox copies of some other stock statements, and the defense could never produce **the original documents as they did not**

exist at all. He further added that the defendant very cunningly used various letters exchanged between him and the bank containing the signatures of Mr. Gokhale. He then prepared the said two statements by Xeroxing the signatures of Mr. Gokhale. Thus it was the matter of forgery. In order to corroborate his argument our advocate further produced a letter from somewhere, that proprietor of ABC was debarred by the University for forging a degree.

I need not say that the case was decided in favour of the bank and all of us had a sigh of relief!

Take Away :
- ➢ **Documents of the bank be guarded properly.**
- ➢ **While putting remarks and signatures take appropriate care.**
- ➢ **Always follow a particular system while creating a record.**
- ➢ **Never loose your heart as the truth always comes out.**
- ➢ **In respect of legal matter always furnish full, complete and truthful information to your advocate.**

• • •

(6) Mr. Dave's Dilemma!

Our Branch Deputy Chief Officer (DCO then in1978, now designated as Scale II Officer) Mr. Dave, sent a message through our head peon, that I should meet him immediately in the cabin. Then the Branch was headed by a Chief Manager, quite a high profile post at that time. I was in the clerical cadre and handling Forex, BG / LC department. Surprisingly on that day my department in charge, the Accountant, the Branch Manager all were absent consequently, Mr. Dave the senior most officer was in charge of the branch. He was to superannuate after a period of 10 months and hence was working over cautiously.

He told me to sit. There I saw Shri Rao who was Head of the

Accounts department of NSW Ltd. one of our reputed clients. I smiled and shook hands with him. Mr. Dave told me that Shri Rao wants a Bank Guarantee of Rs 35 lakhs urgently for his company. He said further that the Company had availed all the facilities and in none of the accounts limits were available. Mr. Rao handed over the requisite documents and left the office saying that he would come back by 4 pm to collect the BG.

Mr. Dave was perplexed, neither could he refuse nor could he go ahead by issuing the concerned BG as he did not have the powers to do so and of course the safe retirement must be looming large in his mind. He was nonplussed because of the situation as he knew the importance and worth of the client on one hand and the wrath he would have to face from the very strict Regional Manager in case of delay or non issue of BG. He said to himself, such an important matter had to crop up today only, when both the top bosses were on leave. He was very jittery and was expecting some solution. He handed over all the requisite documents to me but did not say anything, perhaps not able to decide the action to be taken.

Knowing the importance of the BG, silently I took all the documents in my possession and went to my desk. I prepared the proposal, got the Bank Guarantee and the Counter Guarantee typed in the format, marked the margin deposit under lien. I also prepared all the relevant accounting vouchers and entered the details in the BG register. All these rituals took about two hours and it was 2 pm already. I got up to approach Mr. Dave. But I found him standing before me with a tense face. I requested him to have a seat and informed him that all the procedural matter was complete. The next step was to sanction the BG and execute the BG document. He was restless, unable to decide and perhaps looking for some solution to resolve the difficult situation. I then intervened, saying, 'Sir, do you believe in me?' He had to say yes, as there was no other alternative. He had seen me working in the Forex and BG /LC department for last one and half year though he was never my immediate boss. I then put up all the relevant papers to be signed by him, got his signatures, which he did very hesitantly meekly smiling at me. I took charge of all the papers, kept those in an office bag and informed him that I am going to the Regional Office which was 500 meters away. I saw in his eyes a distinct look of fear, dismay, save me and a question mark!

I straight away went to RO, with a plan in my mind to tackle the situation. I approached the PA of Regional Manager; I told her that I would like to meet RM personally in respect of a BG of NSW Ltd. She knew me very well as in her earlier posting she was attached with our department. She informed me that one client is inside and I can go as soon as he comes out. She asked me where my department in charge was. She also advised me to be careful, 'As you are venturing in a den' she remarked. Yes everybody feared of him, such was his personality.

After few minutes, I knocked, sought permission and then I was standing before him. He gazed at me, perhaps PA might have told him about me. I introduced myself. He gestured at me to go ahead. I briefly told him the urgency to issue BG for NSW Ltd. and also informed that it had been signed by our DCO Mr. Dave. I stated further, 'Sir, this BG needs signature of another authorized signatory and incidentally other authorities at the branch were on leave. The authority at RO, ARM of this office was on tour and there was no second signatory available.' He asked, 'Then what?' I very humbly said Sir, 'Please sign the documents.' He gestured me to show the papers. I was ready with papers properly tagged. He went through them and asked me, 'Where should I sign?' I promptly showed the right place for countersigning. He asked me only one question, 'How long you are working in the department.' I answered, 'Sir about two years.' He smiled at me, gave all papers and told me to leave the copy of BG with PA. I thanked him and ran towards our office, of course after thanking the PA.

It was about 3.30 pm and Mr. Dave was very eagerly waiting for me. When he saw me he literally caught hold of me. He was impatiently waiting to listen to what had happened at Regional Office. I told him the entire episode and then showed him the counter signature of RM on the Bank Guarantee. He was dumb folded and so relieved that he could not even thank me. I could understand how a person on the verge of retirement could get scared.

Of course, after resumption of our Branch Manager, he narrated the entire story to him, including how fearful he was, and then he appreciated and thanked me. Our Branch Manager patted me saying, 'Well done!'

Take Away :
- ➢ **There will be always some sort of problems while working, but if you have desire to look for solutions, you will surely arrive at it.**
- ➢ **Be bold and face the situation.**

• • •

(7) 31ˢᵗ March, A high Powered Drama.

Today on this day of 31ˢᵗ March, 2015, the situation I faced on that closing day flashed back in my mind and once again I shuddered with its remembrance.

For any banker 31ˢᵗ March is one of the most important and busy day. It decides the fate of the Branch Managers, Regional Managers, Zonal Managers, General Managers and even that of the Top Most Executives working in any Bank. It is a day of consolidation, the jugglery a banker has to perform, the acrobatic acts for keeping his asset side strong and also reaching to a reasonable level of profits. Any banker on this D' Day is always in a gloomy mood. I was thinking right from starting from residence to the office, how I will manage the day's work, what things I should handle first, what is the most urgent and important work, whom I must contact which entries I must check and what not? It is the last minute reading or rehearsal before the final yearly examination.

When I left my residence travelling in a car to the office, on that fateful day of 31ˢᵗ March 2011, the same thoughts of managing the show were hovering in my mind. I was in the third world and even could not react to the speed with which I was driven, under the normal conditions I would have pulled the driver at least twice.

We reached near the building located on the back side of the main building of the branch, at Fort, Mumbai where we had temporarily shifted to enable the renovation of *'The Monumental Heritage Building of the Bank.' We were to celebrate The Centenary of the Bank within a span of next nine months and hence we had occupied the present premises. The event of Centenary Celebration being of utmost importance was regularly covered by media.*

On the outskirts an IB Van and some people from media laced with cameras were present, but I hardly noticed them, obviously because at that time my mind must had been occluded with the yearly closing work that I had to attend. And secondly because in that prestigious business area there were houses like Tata's, Videocon's etc where IB van and news personnel were a very common sight.

I entered my very small cabin, which was already occupied by 5 to 6, totally unknown persons. I could sense that the place was engulfed with a strange mystic silence. I occupied my chair at around 10 am. Earlier at the entrance, my head peon had informed me that he had seated some unknown people in my cabin. I was fathoming who these unknown people were, I tried to smile, but I must have failed in my attempt. They were surely not my customers or the auditors or even they did not appear as officials from any Government Office. Then who were they? I was fathoming in my mind but could not reach to any conclusion. They appeared to me as intruder, unwelcome guest on that very important yearly closing day as I would be distracted from very planned activities for that all important day. I remained silent not knowing how to begin. Ultimately the senior most of them broke the excruciating silence by introducing him as the Chairman of a society named ABC, and further he reveled that these three were also the Officials of the society. Taking a pause he furthered his aversion saying that the other 3 gentlemen are bailiff of the court. I was totally confused and at a complete loss when that senior waving a paper told in a very cold voice that they had a court decree and an attachment order to attach the building of Bombay Branch (The said building was our Head Office Building as per information, in the public domain) in respect of a Civil Suit against the bank. I was more confused as there was no such case against my branch i.e. Mumbai office. He then took out the court decree, attachment order and was looking towards the court bailiff. They responded saying that they are ready to paste the order and take possession of the building. For few seconds I was numb, but quickly gathered my thoughts and asked for the orders. The court orders were exactly the same as told, but on going through the decree I understood that, it was in respect of a **civil suit for vacating the premises filed against some other local branch** few years ago. The speaking court orders contained a decree for Mesne profit to the tune of Rs100 lakhs (rounded of), since the concerned branch had not paid the claimed rent. In fact Mumbai Branch was not concerned at all what so ever happened and was oblivious about the case.

Now they were very anxious to attach the Mumbai Main Office building perhaps being not treated properly by the concerned branch authority in the past. There was a tint of vengeance in their action. They had come fully prepared with the photographers, news personnel, an IB van to shoot the action and relevant court orders at their hands. It was a perfect 'Breaking News' which would be live broadcast throughout the nation! I could imagine the catastrophe that would follow.

The Bank was continuously broadcasting the beginning *of 'The Centenary Year' and* during this period if the *'The Monumental Heritage Building of the Bank'* was attached one can imagine the tumultuous effect on the name and fame of the bank and as a consequence the wrath and suffering the concerned Branch Manager had to undergo.

On weighing all these aspects and clearly understanding the effect it would have on the reputation of the Bank, I slowly but firmly told the Decree holders that concerned paltry amount of Rs. 100 lakhs would be paid by me through a Bankers Cheque. So there was absolutely no question of attachment of the prestigious building. I said this with great conviction that whatever I was doing was to save the reputation, name and fame of the bank and against which an amount of Rs 100 lakhs has no meaning. I took that instantaneous decision without hitch and with awareness that I do not have the relevant powers to pay such amount. But prestige of my bank was utmost than any other aspect. Further I called one of my close and experienced Senior Officers to prepare the relevant Bankers' Cheque. He was an intelligent officer had closely observing the episode had understood the gravity thereof. He smartly said Sir, our system starts at 11 am and we would require another 15 minutes for making the Bankers' Cheque, understanding that this would fetch some time. The Chairman who was sitting very upright and speaking in a very authoritative and arrogant tone, now buckled down, looking dismayed. Then I asked the Chairman that since I am depositing the money in compliance to the court decree, he should ask all those news personnel to disperse. He also thought that the matter has been settled, it was wise to comply with my request to save his skin. Those people dispersed in no time.

My next move was definitely to obtain proper sanction from higher authorities as well to obtain the legal advice. On the pretext of going to the wash room I spoke with our Law Officer located in Zonal Office which was at a stone's throw distance and I narrated the entire episode.

Then addressing to all and particularly towards the bailiff, I said, 'You must have started very early in the morning from the residence and would not have even taken your breakfast. We have a very good restaurant just besides our branch, let us go and have some breakfast.' Saying this I started. All got up and hesitantly followed me. In fact, I wanted to while away some time so that our Law Officer would get sufficient time to get information from the concerned branch, RO and of course, the advocate who was handling the case at civil court. After the breakfast all of us went to Zonal Office on the pretext of completing the formalities of handing over the Bankers' Cheque. In the mean time the Legal Officer had collected all the information and obtained the sanction from the competent Higher Authorities.

Ultimately the BC was handed over at around 5 pm, after complying with certain formalities as suggested by our Higher

Authorities and then only I had a sigh of relief as the *'high powered drama'* ended for me.

You can imagine the plight I had to suffer as the entire day was lost!

(I did not have any information about the present status of the case.)

Take Away :

➢ **How an important matter translates into an urgent one if not addressed to, at a proper time.**

➢ **Decision making is an art; it involves the choice of the best option out of the viable ones.**

➢ **Remember, though it is essential to plan the day, certain urgent, unavoidable matters may always crop up for which you must have a Plan B.**

➢ **In a catastrophic situation take a long breath; give some moments to your gray cells in the brain to think and to decide.**

• • •

(8) Ganesh Pooja

Tomorrow will be the beginning of Ganesh festival and hence today the entire Mumbai was in that fervor. The Ganesh idols were being brought in processions with the usual traditional festivities. All the roads were full of people, vehicles, trucks, tractors and the people were in the religious mood. I too had started from office at exactly 5 pm, but to reach home it took me four hours instead of usual two hours. On reaching home after dinner, I too had decorated the place for tomorrow's pooja. Around 10.30 pm I was preparing to go to bed, when I received a call. It was from Mr. Mhatre, our Cashier; he was speaking from International Airport. I was amazed, as they had started from our Branch as usual at 3.30 pm with foreign currency in the banks'cash van with security guards.

Our branch was extending a special service to one of our very old clients, a Foreign Exchange dealer of exporting the foreign currency like US $, Pound Sterling etc. The usual method was to check the Currency Notes, pack them in a particular way. Prepare the documents for Export and after clearance by the Customs Authority hand it over to the designated courier under proper receipt. Next day the receipt would be checked and the usual accounting entries would be passed. Generally all these procedure would take around 3 hours and our entire remittance team of 5 to 6 persons would be free by at most 7 pm. This routine was going on for years.

Mr. Mhatre informed me that it took them around six hours to reach the air port Customs Office as they were stuck up at various junctions on the road because of the Ganesh Procession as well the usual road was closed because of visit of some VVIP. Then on reaching Customs Office at about 10 pm they found that the usual Custom's Officer had left a bit early. They waited for the other Officer to report to the duty up to 10.30 pm. But now they were informed that he would report only at 11 pm and since it was already 10.30 pm they were unable to undertake the usual job as their rules do not permit the same. Even after repeated requests they were not listening. Sir, you please try to convince them and he handed over the mobile phone to the person on duty, who very reluctantly answered. I tried to communicate the difficulties to him and appealed him to help us once. I had some contacts with Officers of the department and tried to leverage them, but he was in no mood even to listen to our repeated requests. He did not budge and handed back the mobile. It means some other solution had to be found. Had it been other cities I would have called back the Key Holding Officers of the Cash Department and re-deposited the Currency. But this option was not viable in Mumbai, since it would have taken several hours, perhaps the next day. Then tomorrow it was the Ganesh Pooja, a holiday and the next day was Sunday.

It was nearing 11.30 pm. I was pondering in my mind what could be the safest possible solution? An idea struck to my mind,

I told Mr. Mahtre to wait there for some time as I knew, and it was a safe place. At that hour I gauged the list of contacts on my mobile and found the mobile number of the Manager of the firm for whom we were remitting the currency. And Yes, I thanked God that I got the number and the concerned Manager replied after about 8 to 10 rings at the very odd hours. He did recognize me instantly as we used to speak frequently. He was also dazed to listen the whole story, but nonplussed perhaps because he was too sleepy. He remained silent for few seconds, not knowing what to do under such difficult situation. I furthered the talk by asking him, whether we could do something with their Safe Lockers available at Domestic Airport. His voice was immediately responsive as some solution was in the air. He told that he would speak with their representative at the Domestic Airport, since they do receive the couriers from other places in the night and deposit the same at their Airport Safe, I would come back, he said and put down. I also anxiously waited for his telephone and did receive the positive response after few minutes. He gave me the full details of the place of their office cum safe lockers and person to be contacted at the Domestic Airport. In return I communicated all the details and steps to be taken by Mr. Mahtre, our cashier, who incidentally knew the concerned person at the Domestic Airport. Fortunately the International Airport and the Domestic Airport at Mumbai are at a distance of only few Kilometers.

Since having played my part of the job in the drama there was nothing to do except to wait, I opened a book and started reading. After the passage of about an hour I received a call from Mr. Mhatre. He was now speaking in a very relaxed tone. He confirmed that currency was accepted by the representative Mr. Sharan and as directed he and the other person of the firm had duly acknowledged the receipt as usual. I thanked him and other staff i.e. the driver, two guards and the sub staff. 'Sir, I was sure, you would find some solution' said, Shri Chavan one of the Security guards.

The next day had already begun as I approached the bed at

about 2 am, but with full of peace and satisfaction.

On the next 26ᵗʰ January, we felicitated all the members of the Team at the hands of the then General Manager (the ZM of the Zone).

Take Away :

> ➤ **A Manager is one who knows very well all the activities carried out under the roof.**

> ➤ **Always keep a rapport with important and the key persons working for your Customers.**

• • •

Confronting Difficult Situations

One day or the other, a Manager has to face crises or difficult situations in the business life and has to manage at different levels. But he must possess an attitude of, *'Never say give up' or 'Never say die.'* Rather under the difficult situations only your courage and managerial / leadership skills are tested. In such situations remember you are always alone, everywhere there would be darkness and there will be no colleagues to support you. If you are feeling discouraged, nervous and no light in the sight at the end of a tunnel, you should not reveal it, neither to your colleagues nor to your staff because it may create a gloom and may discourage others. As such in such trying conditions also one has to **show** happiness and a positive attitude. ***In fact not only to show these Attitudes but it should flow from the Bottom of the Heart. This is the Hallmark of a True Leader.***

• • •

7 | Facing Angry Customers

(1) The Buddha !

'Madam now only 2 minutes are remaining', watching the big clock on the wall and simultaneously his wrist watch Mr. Zaveri was warning the concerned lady CTO handling the Savings Department with anger in his eyes and in a loud voice. I was watching the client from my cabin. He was fourth in the line and earlier had asked the madam how much time she would take to complete the entries and printing the Pass book for his Savings account. Sir, wait for Five minutes was her reply. She somehow managed to handover the Pass Book to the gentleman!

There was a repetition of the same episode exactly after about six months. He was then pacified by one of the colleagues of the CTO.

It was a very busy Monday as the Bank was closed for last two days and being the first week of the Month. There were at least 8 to10 customers in line waiting to be served on every counter. Our gentleman customer, Mr. Zaveri arrived and stood in the line at the Saving Bank Counter. He was restless as there were 7 customers ahead of him. He waited for about 2 minutes and asked in a loud voice from there only, 'How much time it would take?' The concerned lady CTO replied, Sir 'Wait for 15 minutes.' After few minutes he warned in his usual style, 'Madam, your 12 minutes are already over and still four customers are ahead of me.' Somebody tried to pacify him by saying that look madam was working. But he started complaining that the Bank is not having a separate counter for senior and important citizens like me. CTO was facing some problem with the Printer and hence the Savings in charge was trying to rectify it. Mr. Zaveri flared up and said loudly what sort of the printer the Bank was providing. In fact it was the best quality printer and the officer soon got it alright. Mr. Zaveri started abusing the service provided by the branch. I immediately got out and requested him to calm down and sit inside for a moment. He furiously started addressing at me, 'I am the owner of the Bank and you are absolutely incompetent and should be dismissed. I am going to complain against you and your staff with your Regional Office, Zonal Office and CMD of the Bank.' He was disturbing the smooth functioning of the branch on such a busy day for nothing and creating a scene. Somehow me and one of the sub staff who knew him for years was successful in bringing him inside my cabin. However he was reluctant to sit. I also stood up. A glass of water was brought for him but he denied. He was still angry and asked for a paper perhaps to write a complaint. I did give him a paper and a pen to write down. In the mean time the Officer got his work done and handed over his 5 Pass books and a cheque book which he took reluctantly. It took about 10 minutes to calm him down and then only he drank a glassful of cold water. He left grumbling something with himself, perhaps next time I would definitely complain. Factually it had taken only 20 minutes to provide him the service on a busy day which was good at any standards.

It was a Saturday and clock was showing 2 pm - our closing time. I was passing near our locker room and observed that an aged lady was sitting opposite to our Officer handling lockers. He introduced, 'Sir, Mrs. Savitriben one of our good old customers.' I smiled and said 'Namaste'. She said 'I am waiting for my husband as we had to attend a marriage tomorrow, we would like to operate the locker for collecting some articles.' In a minute somebody came out and they got inside for locker operations. After few minutes our gentleman customer Mr. Zaveri was standing against me, looking angrily he spoke, 'Now even your lockers are having problems. Do you undertake the usual cleaning and oiling of the lockers? My locker is not opening?' I just pointed with a gesture to go to his locker and he followed me reluctantly. Oh, so Mrs. Savitriben was his wife. When we reached the locker I requested him, 'Shall I try once with your key?' He very reluctantly handed over the key. Just a touch and a look at the key and I immediately informed him, 'Sir, you had brought the wrong KEY! It was perhaps the key of locker of some other Bank.' Mrs. Savitriben pulled him in Gujarati and looking at me said, 'He still cannot come out from his earlier role. Tomorrow we have to go to attend a marriage and the ornaments are necessary'. Now Mr. Zavari was looking at me perhaps for some support. I told my locker officer to wait for an hour though locker timings were up to 2 pm only. Mr. Zavari came back with proper key by 2.45 pm, operated the locker, Ben thanked me and left smiling.

After a period of about 3 months, as per transfer orders, I was to report to a new place. Sitting late evening I was looking for some papers when our reputed customer and my good friend Shri Bhat arrived in my office. We warmly wished each other. Looking outside the cabin, he called someone and addressed, 'Sir, here is Mr. Zaveri, an Ex Secretary to State Government, Ministry of Commerce. He referred Mr. Zaveri, 'Mr. Gokhale has changed the entire working of the branch. His branch has been rated as the best branch of the area and had the highest growth.' Then he gave me a Bouquet and best wishes for my new assignment!

Mr. Zaveri very meekly told Mr. Bhat, 'I know Mr. Gokhale' and tried to smile. And then he took out a carefully wrapped packet, Sir, 'With good wishes!'

Next day after the prayer, I told the staff about the yesterday's meeting and then as per popular demand opened the packet. Wow! Was the response from everybody.

It was *An Extremely Beautiful Bust of 'The Buddha.'*

'Sir, of all the Branch Managers you are the only one who won over Mr. Zaveri', said one of the staff members and all joined him!

Take Away :

➢ Remember some customers merely complain just to get their ego satisfied and for attracting the attention and recognition.

➢ Never fall into a trap of retaliation.

➢ In a scuffle with a customer; if you win and customer loses, you lose the customer; if you lose and customer wins, you again lose the customer. As such always arrive at a win-win solution.

• • •

(2) Shri Kakaji

I was preparing to leave office at around 4.30 pm for some urgent meeting at Zonal Office, when Shri Kakaji entered my cabin shouting and throwing hands in the air. He was literally trembling with anger. I stood up, requesting him to have a sit and offered a glass of water. When I asked him, 'What was the matter?' He was very furious and with clenched feasts told me, 'The dealing lady officer was not competent and did not handle the customers properly. She did not comply with the instructions given by aged customer like me.' I was repeatedly requesting him to calm down and sit. But he was so infuriated and flared up, because I was not calling the officer as demanded by him, but he thought that I am deliberately shielding her. In fact I did not have any knowledge as to what had happened. I requested him again to understand what the problem was. Instead of telling me, he was so out of mind and agitated that he literally took his **Chappal** (footware) in hand to strike me. The situation was terrible. However I remained calm and composed and again and again requesting him with folded hands to calm down. In the bout of anger he was shaking like a tremor but ultimately could not control himself and melted down and literally fell in the chair, totally exhausted. I caught one of his hands and patted him and asked him to drink some water. He was profusely perspiring and was fully drenched with sweat. I urgently called my PA to summon the doctor who was incidentally in the branch. His BP had shot up. Doctor checked him and gave a shot of medicine and a pill. After gulping a pill and passage of some time he was quite normal. When he became normal, he was so ashamed that he bowed down to touch my feet to say sorry. He was humbly requesting me to forgive him as he had totally lost control over self.

To divert attention I just changed the topic and asked him about the health of his ailing wife. He said to me that he was still feeling extremely nervous for his action and could not understand how he had done that shameful act. On my asking again about the health of his wife; with great pains reflecting on his face, he informed me that as per opinion of expert doctors there is remote possibility of her recovery.

I assured him that I had forgotten everything and already wiped off the unfortunate incidence from my memory.

The concerned lady officer was watching everything from outside through the glass pane, but did not have courage to come inside. When she saw that the situation has calmed down she came inside and apologized to Shri Kakaji that his instructions could not be complied with.

The matter was that Shri Kakaji at about 2 pm had given 4 Export Bills for US $ 40000 to be purchased on that day. Those were to be booked in the system to complete purchase transaction and to be accounted for, before 3 pm i.e. the time of closure of Forex transactions. Shri Kakji had prior information that US $ would crash by the end of the day and next 2 days were the holidays. She was unable to book the entry in the system because of some technical problem and hence transaction could not pass through on that day. As expected by Shri Kakaji, U S $ slipped from Rs.63 to Rs.61.75 by 4 pm and hence he was angry.

We explained him the circumstances why we were unable to close the transaction on the day. I further assured him that as a special case we would take up the matter with higher authorities and compensate him to the maximum possible extent.

It may be added that the account of the firm was with bank

for over 60 years and opened by Shri Kakaji's father. Kakaji was then 78 years old.

Next day we visited the hospital to enquire about the health of the ailing wife of Shri Kakaji and offered her a nice Bouquet and some fruits.

The bank authorities granted some concession to the satisfaction of Shri Kakaji to compensate a part of loss and the episode ended with a win-win situation. During my recent visit to the branch I learnt about the sad demise of Kakaji, but was satisfied to learn that the third generation of the said family firm is still proudly dealing with us.

Take Away :

➢ **Remember the Relationships are to be handled with great care.**

➢ **Always try to find a win-win solution.**

➢ **If a customer is a fire ball you must be a cool snow ball.**

➢ **When a person is very angry, his mind is occluded, then he cannot think rationally and this results into mad bouts.**

➢ **Customers' want... To express their emotions. Have their problem solved. To be heard.**

● ● ●

(3) A Withdrawl Form

One of my colleagues was working on a Savings Bank counter and it was a usual day. One of the clients produced a pass book and a withdrawal form to draw from the account. The ledger keeper on going through the withdrawal form observed some lacunae and very un-intentionaly, he gave another one to be rewritten and tore the wrong one. He had observed that in place of name, amount was written and vice a versa. The person who had produced the with-drawl form was very angry and loudly protested, why the form was torn into pieces? Nobody understood what had happened and the cause of eruption. The other colleague immediately came forward and asked how much he would like to withdraw, but he was more infuriated. Then he asked what authority you had to destroy the form. Still for us it was a very simple matter to fill another form. Then he retorted, 'Who will sign?' Our faces were speaking, 'Why? Obviously you.' He was disgusted and said, we had very urgent requirement and as such Babuji had given this form yesterday and left for his hometown, which was in the different State. Now how am I to attend the job?

Our branch accountant called him and asked him to sit down. He was also not clear and asked for the details. The gentleman replied, 'Babuji (father) had given this form and passbook for meeting certain urgent expenses and your staff had torn the form. Now how I would settle the bills of the doctor and the chemist? Since Babuji is out of station new form cannot be signed and now, how I can receive the money?' Our accountant pacified him, and then asked the sub staff to collect all the pieces lying in the dust bin and to paste all the parts on a single sheet. Then on reverse side, he took the signature of that gentleman and facilitated the payment. The gentlemen left with a smile.

Take Away :

➤ **Sometimes even an innocent action can also create problems.**

• • •

(4) A Hot Potato

I was working on an important credit proposal, when I heard shouting outside the cabin. There was a scuffle going on between one of our CTO's and one young customer. The Customer was shouting with anger and was threatening that he would telephone and call the police. He was very loudly protesting, 'I am going to lodge a complaint against you for misbehaving with my wife under

Atrocities against Women's act. It appeared to be a very serious matter.

One of the lady customers signed a cheque and gave it to the CTO for encashment. The CTO informed her that it cannot be honoured since it was not signed by the authorised person. She informed that the cheque was for a joint account with her husband and hence she had signed as a drawer it should be honoured. The CTO told her that she cannot draw the cheque and asked her to get it signed from her husband so that it can be cashed. She insisted for cashing and he again told her the same, perhaps in a bit loud tone. She felt intimidated and telephoned to her husband and informed that the CTO was refusing the payment and misbehaved with her and he should come to the branch immediately. All this happened in about two minutes and the concerned in-charge of savings department had no time to act. Her husband was present there in no time. He spoke angrily and in a high pitch, 'How you dared to speak with my wife rudely and refused payment?' On this, CTO answered, 'I told her to get your signature on the cheque and never refused the payment.' He complained, 'You did not have any authority to refuse her signature on the withdrawal and I strongly condemn speaking with her in a rude way.' CTO informed that the account was a joint one and there were no instructions for operation by his wife. He retorted, 'Your branch had paid her at least ten times'. Again he protested and loudly said, 'I am going to call Police and lodge the complaint.' He started dialing. He was speaking with full throttle. The situation was like a **'steaming potato'** in hand. Myself and one of our customers Shri Rahi reached the spot simultaneously. There was an absolute silence from all others as nobody comprehended the drama going on inside the counter for last few minutes. Shri Rahi and one of the sub staff members, perhaps acquainted with the angry customer and myself somehow managed to direct him to my cabin. He was fuming, but Shri Rahi and we calmed him and arranged for a glass of water. He angrily asked me for a paper and pen. On producing it, he addressed Shri Rahi, **'Aap nahi hote to mai use do thappad lagata'** (I would have slapped him). He was confused, what to write in his complaint.

I apologised, for the inconvenience caused to him and for the improper words or insult to his wife by our staff. No-no nothing wrong from you but I will complain. Shri Rahi said 'Mr.Yadav I know you and also the CTO closely. He is a good chap. There may be some misunderstanding and we will sort it out. 'Your CTO must apologise to my wife for his misbehavior' said, Mr. Yadav.

The ladies staff on their level made the complainant's wife comfortable. The payment was also arranged. We took operational instructions, 'Either or Survivor' for his account and it was recorded. We called for cold drinks and I enquired about his business. He was engaged in transport business. I assured him to help him in his business when required. When I found that the Complainant was quite cool and composed I called my CTO. He very sportingly apologized. The root cause of the episode was not obtaining the proper operational instructions. I thanked Mr. Rahi for his timely help.

I did warn our CTO that he should be more polite while speaking with the lady customers.

Take Away :

Customer Emotions

> **An angry or frustrated customer will not respond easily to logic, so emotions must be addressed first.**
> **Say: 'I am so sorry that you are upset' or 'I understand why you are frustrated.'**
> **Don't judge on one instance of acting with 'jerk'; judge others fairly as you would do with yours.**

• • •

(5) Nagpur Connection

'This is General Manager Sahu speaking', I answered 'Good Noon Sir!' GM said, 'I was with CMD and he was very upset as a very nasty mail was received by him and that too from a very high profiled customer Mr. A, who you must be aware, was second in command of TATA Group. He forwarded the mail to me and told me the crux. Mr. A had stated that few days back he had approached the branch and informed the locker officer that he was in need of a large size locker. Since it was not readily available as informed, he had requested to record his demand in the register. A locker of his choice was vacated by some customer. However instead of issuing the locker to him as per system, his demand was over looked by the locker officer and issued it to an Executive of the bank, over riding his legitimate claim. He was very much upset because of this and he had very bitterly mentioned that it means your Bank treats an Executive of the Bank more important and valuable than a very old customer like me. 'He had protested the action of the bank without mincing the words in a very pungent manner and directly alleged the bank.'

When I read and understood the episode I too was shocked, as I had no knowledge. In fact in case of a Branch Manager of a very large branch such operational transaction was the responsibility of the concerned Officer. Of course for any happening under the roof of a branch is a vicarious liability of the BM. I had to go ahead with immediate damage control action. First I visited the safe deposit lockers, verified the records and after discussion with the staff found that what was claimed by Mr. A was true. The Officer had given preference to the Executive of the bank while allotting the locker. It was observed that no locker to suit the requirement was available. In fact big lockers are always in demand but short in supply as they were not generally surrendered. I did not tell anything about the complaint to the locker in charge, but I had a hunch that he had some knowledge. Simultaneously, I instructed the Officer to inform me if any locker is surrendered. I also told him to look out for any possibility of the requisite locker surrendered through our contacts. Since there were two other branches in the 2 to 3 Km periphery of our branch I had contacted the Branch Managers and reserved the similar type of lockers with them.

The next obvious step was to call on Mr. A personally and tackle the situation. In the mean time our GM called on the branch and he contacted the PA of Mr. A, for appointment. Fortunately, PA and our GM belonged to the same place and hence he responded positively and some groundwork was done by me. I got the vital information that Mr. A belonged to my native place and he had worked with TISCO at Tatanagar.

We could get the appointment only at 4 pm on next Sunday that is after five excruciating days. I had to take action against the erring Officer. I also received a call from much worried ZM, seeking from me the steps taken in this case as he also got the message. I informed him the steps taken by me and about the proposed meeting. Some action was needed against the erring Officer. So I requested the ZM to transfer the said Officer urgently to some other branch. It was done. I got vital information from a sub staff working in the locker department that one of our staff also had a similar type of locker. He also confirmed that the episode as described had happened.

On the meeting day I reached the office in the afternoon and telephoned to our GM at about 3 pm to remind him about the meeting. One of my CM was also present just to support me and for backing if required as he had contacts with other Tata Executives.

We went in the cabin. I introduced myself and our GM and straight way we apologized Mr. A, for the behaviour of our branch Officer and also said that we respect our customers and for them we have highest value and regards. Mr. A retorted, 'But your action does not reflect it. He further expressed his anguish.' I informed to Mr. A, 'Sir, we have arranged two similar types of lockers in nearby branches at a distance of around 2 Km.' But he straight away denied and said, 'I want it at your branch only.' We further suggested that we can provide two smaller size lockers, which he did not accept. Our GM also tried to convince him in different ways by telling that he was the emissary of CMD. He was not yielding, though he was keeping the discussion in a very polite way. For a change I asked, Sir, 'Are you also from Nagpur, it is my native place.' The question had a magnetic effect and his eyes glittered, 'Yes-yes. It is my birth place and we had a parental house there and I was also schooled there.' We did speak about the common contacts. 'Sir, I learnt that you were at Jamshedpur in TISCO and must be knowning Late Mr. Moolgaonkar (Head of Finance and Accounts).' 'Oh very well!' I then continued, 'Sir, and then you may had acquaintance with Late Mr. Limaye. His face light up and he quipped, 'Mr. Limaye who was Chief Engineer?' But how come you know him? Sir, 'He was my maternal uncle.' Now he heartily smiled. We felt the change in his stance and we felt a bit relived.

He then continued, 'Mr. Gokhale, arrange for a Locker of my requirement soon.' We assured him. He said, 'However I am presently not withdrawing my letter.' We thanked him and left.

My GM was happy that ice was broken and he appreciated my **Nagpur Connection,** 'It was like a magic wand,' he said.

The immediate task was to provide him a locker as fast as possible.

I was pursued by the higher ups to take immediate disciplinary action against the Officer, but I knew he was to retire in ensuing month and hence I was going slow and transferred his services out of Region.

Then I called my staff member who had the requisite locker, explained the entire case and requested her if she could surrender the locker and instead occupy two smaller lockers. After a bit of persuasion she agreed. Next day she surrendered the locker and I telephoned Mr. A to inform him that locker is arranged. 'I would send my daughter and wife on Friday. Please keep it reserved for me.'

In the mean time I got another cue from my sub staff that the next i.e. on Wednesday Mrs. J, wife of Mr. A would be celebrating her birthday! What an important feed back? I immediately ordered for a nice bouquet and a box of Chocolates to be reached to their house.

On Friday Mrs. J with her daughter and daughter in law Mr. M visited the branch; they were welcomed and issued the requisite locker. All of them thanked me; Mr. M was so impressed that he assured me to start a Current Account of their Limited Company in our branch.

After two days, I received a nicely drafted letter of satisfaction from Mr. A. Our concerned Executive had superannuated in the earlier month.

The Inquiry was completed in due course and the concerned Officer was punished with 'A Warning!' He also retired from Bank service after putting in 38 years of service.

Take Away :

> **When we are wrong do not hesitate to apologize.**
> **Always remember to leverage the Customers personal information.**
> **Utilise every opportunity to reach to the customer.**
> **Be on the side of the staff if they have not done wrong.**
> **Make sure that the conflict is resolved and the relationship is leveraged to secure business.**

• • •

'Do You Know Why Customers Leave?'

Reasons for Exit
1 % Death
3 % Move Away
5 % Develop Other Relationship
9 % Leave for Competitive Reasons
14 % Dissatisfied with Product or Service
68 % Leave because of Rude behaviour or Discourteous Service

Monitor your Stress Level

New York Times ranked the ten most stressful occupations of which five are!

1. Police officers.
2. Fire fighters
3. Air traffic controllers.
4. Road Traffic Police
5. First Line Banking Staff

(This stressful position was compounded in organizations that treated their employees poorly. These employees, unfortunately, go on to treat their customers poorly by unloading their frustrations onto them.)

Key to Handle Angry/Challenging (Difficult) Customers

1. Customers Emotions

- Address emotions first.
- Help the customer focus.
- Keep yourself and your customer focused.
- Set limits on customer behaviour.
- An angry or frustrated customer will not respond easily to logic, so emotions must be addressed first.
- Say: 'I am so sorry that you are upset' or 'I understand why you are frustrated.'

2. Defuse the Anger

- Studies show that if emotions are addressed for about **16 seconds** before responding to their complaint, they will usually calm down.
- Prior to diffusing your customer's anger, make sure you have your own anger under control
- Do not respond with anger to anger or with stress to stress.
- Pay attention to the behaviour of the customer.
- Be professional, polite and direct. Model the mood you want them to adopt, cool and calm.
- Involve the customer in the decision making process by asking for what the customer would do or suggest.

3. Keep Yourself and Your Customer Focussed

- Know what you want to know and what your customer wants?

- Learn to be flexible.

4. Communicate Effectively

- Speak in a way that calms.
- Build rapport.
- Send the right nonverbal messages.
- Ensure your grasp of the problem.

5. Project a Professional Image

- Neat, clean, good appearance. Eye contact, warm, open and friendly stance.
- Tone of your voice will reflect how you're feeling are. Strive to sound calm. Practice it with friends and your family!
- A few well chosen words can be music to your customers' ears. Keep a list close by and practice:-'I am so sorry'~ 'Please, let me help you', or 'Let's sit down to talk'.

6. Assert yourself

- Be confident and direct but not aggressive. Otherwise you will lose credibility!
- In case of Letters/Emails use proper grammar, punctuation and wording.
  Never send out an emotionally charged communiqué; you cannot take it back!

7. Pass the Difficult Customer to someone else!

This will only make the customer more upset~
Remember the saying 'what goes around comes around...'.
Others may then pass their difficult clients to you!

• • •

8 | Applying Managerial Skills and Techniques

(1) Operation, 81 Cheques

It was a Tuesday and we had been to a nearby village for pre-inspection. Though our branch was an urban branch, six villages were attached to it and I was there on the usual monthly visit along with the Agriculture Officer.

There was a telephone call, and I answered, 'Hello! Hello! This is Gokhale speaking'. On the other side Mr. Thakur, Assistant Branch Manager was speaking and there was urgency in his voice. 'Sir, there is some exigent matter in the branch and hence please come back as soon as possible'. He did not inform what the matter was. But his shaky voice was reflecting that the things were beyond his grasp.

From last week we had begun the work of converting the manual branch to the fully computerized branch. In order to facilitate the computerization, the branch was undergoing a total face lift in the existing furniture and all other requisite interior work. As such simultaneously the jobs relating to electrification, data cabling, air-conditioning and painting were going on. On last Monday we had received around 35-40 cartons containing the CPU, Monitors, Printers, Key boards, Server, Batteries, UPS, other computer accessories, AC unit, fire extinguishers and other gadgets. Teams from software and hardware companies were busy opening the boxes, connecting the gadgets, testing and installing them. Simultaneously furniture and electrical work was also going on. Thus there was lot of hustle and bustle going on in the branch along with the usual busy first week business of the month.

I informed to my colleague about the SOS message received from the branch and we started back. On way back, I was contemplating what could be the reason for the urgent telephone call? Could it be related with the ongoing furnishing work? But then, so far as renovation activities were concerned everything was in place and going on smoothly as planned. We reached the branch at around 12.30 pm.

On reaching the branch Mr. Thakur informed, 'Sir, yesterday Smt. J had recorded a bunch of 81 cheques drawn on various banks, in our Shroff Register (A register for writing the details of cheques drawn on other banks to be lodged in clearing house) amounting to Rs 112.50 lakhs to be sent for next day's clearing and kept in the cupboard as usual. However, this morning when the concerned lady CTO took out the Register she could not find the bunch of cheques. We searched for the bunch of cheques right from 9.45 am, still the bunch could not be traced up to 11.45 am and hence I requested you to come back. These cheques were to be lodged in clearing house at the scheduled time of 1 pm at State Bank of Hyderabad (SBH). 'Sir,' he continued, 'We had searched all 25 cupboards, each and every drawer of all the staff members. To eliminate possibility we had even taken out all the drawers from the hinges inside the tables, but the search was futile. All the tin boxes meant for Cash remittance, the dispatch box and even the Cash Safe was checked but search yielded no results. We had also thoroughly searched all the waste paper baskets and even the gunny bags for trash as well as the place of throwing the trash, 'The Kachara Kundi'(west disposal container) of Municipal Corporation but in vain. We had also checked all those 40 odd boxes received and emptied yesterday. We thus tried all the possible places where there was even a remote chance of getting the missing bunch. Sir, after all unsuccessful attempts we called you.'

We once again repeated the whole exercise of searching the

bunch at all the possible places. Similarly with the help of The Health Department of the Corporation, we searched the site where the garbage was ultimately disposed off. But the last straw also failed as the entire repeat exercise was also unsuccessful and all of us felt defeated. Matter took the very serious turn and it was imperative to take the urgent steps as the Clearing House time was fast approaching.

We decided to participate in the Clearing House transactions of the day and furnish a letter to the house informing all the bankers about misplaced cheques. It was also decided that each participating banker would also be given a separate letter furnishing the available details from the Shroff Register requesting the concerned banks to note caution against the cheques.

An afternoon meeting of all the staff members was arranged to discuss the issue and to have a broader view of the problem to find the solution so that the issue can be resolved. The different views expressed during the meeting by the staff members were

(1) To inform RO and take appropriate action against the concerned staff member.

(2) To contact all the beneficiaries of the cheques and inform them about the loss and seek duplicate from them.

(3) To get information about the drawer of all the cheques and try to obtain duplicate thereof from them.

(4) To wait and watch the situation.

The first suggestion was rejected as it would not yield the desired results; second and the fourth suggestions were found to be unviable. Hence it was unanimously decided to accept the third suggestion. Our Assistant Branch Manager proposed that in order to handle the difficult task all powers may be given to the Branch Manager and each and every staff should support him. One and all agreed to this and expressed their solidarity as this may least affect the concerned staff member. I took promise from them that whatever may come, they would be on my side and would abide by any orders from me as the situation was grievous. First, I sought a letter from the concerned staff member explaining the episode of loss of cheques. Though, other staff members were not agree to this, the defaulting lady staff did give the letter. I assured her that I would do everything possible to protect her, as she had intentionally not done anything.

The details of the lost cheques were somewhat similar to the following table.

Beneficiary of cheque/Drafts	No of instruments	Amount in Lakh Rupees
LIC of India	42	6.00 lakhs
Recd from Mumbai in Quick Cheques Collection. High Value	06	94. 00 lakhs
Saving Account Holders of our branch	05	1.20 lakhs
Current Account Holders of our branch	12	5.30 lakhs
Cheques from other branches recd. For collection	05	4.60 lakhs
DD recd by us from other Banks towards Collection	05	0.20 lakhs
New India Assurance Co	03	1.00 lakhs
United India Assurance Co	03	0.20 lakhs
Total	**81**	**112.50 lakhs**

The 81 lost instruments were of varied nature that is drawn by Individuals / Firms / Companies; DD's of the PSU and Cooperative banks ;Cheques issued by NRI, Treasury, Post Office, Insurance Companies etc.

During the first meeting it was decided that all lady staff members would undertake the responsibility to handle the routine work with the assistance of two Officers and rest of the 6 male staff members and myself would go ahead with the planned work. Three teams were formed named BNK, SHIV and SS to tackle the situation effectively. The important steps to be undertaken and the time schedule fixed were written down -

Steps	Time	Remarks
1 A letter to be given to the Clearing house giving full details about cheques.	Day-one	Done
2 Individual letters to all the bankers giving the cheque numbers and amount, with a request to record stop payment.	Day-one	Done
3 Teams would move to the clearing Branch of each bank and find out which branch had issued the cheque and who is the drawer of the cheque.	Three to Five days	10 Days
4 To visit the concerned branch of the bank along with the letter, to note down the stop payment of the cheque in the account. Obtain the letter from the branch having noted the stop payment in the account. Also seek the details of the drawer such as name, address, telephone number. If possible arrange a telephone call from the branch to the drawer requesting to issue a duplicate cheque.	One month	Two months
5 To visit the drawer (Cheque issuer), give the letter from the drawee bank branch, furnish the drawer an indemnity letter if required and seek a duplicate cheque.	Two months	Three months

It was also decided to meet every day to take review of the situation.

Having prepared a time bound programme for recovery of cheques, our teams moved for action. I communicated the misplacement of the cheques to The Regional Manager over telephone on the very day of the happening. He was very much upset and communicated his displeasure without mincing words. He also asked to serve a memo to the erring staff. Fortunately the RM knew me for years and hence after listening to his anguish, I assured him that I would handle the matter efficiently. The main concern was that the beneficiaries of the instruments should get the payment and there should not be complaints from any quarters and also there should not be any loss of prestige of the branch/ Bank. 'Sir, we are working with all these things in mind and let me assure you that we are confident that we will handle the difficult situation in the most efficient manner. Sir, we need your support and backing, and request you that in case there is any complainant, please assure the complainant that it would be resolved. We would keep you abreast of the situation from time to time.' I further informed that we had formed teams and each and every staff had taken up the challenge. 'Sir at this juncture I do not desire to take any action against the erring staff, as there was no wrongful intention and it would also hamper our efforts and the spirit created amongst the staff of the branch.' He agreed but warned us again for action if there were no results.

Having done the ground work, there was an urgent need to proceed. We decided to begin our task from the cheques issued in favour of LIC of India and the two Insurance companies as there was possibility of the expiry of the Insurance cover in case of non realization of the cheques/DDs and then the onus would be on the bank. The account of LIC was canvassed by us only in the last month and it was snatched from other PSU bank on the assurance of yielding them the best possible service. Under such circumstances our position was more precarious since the cheques were missing. As the Branch Manager of LIC was known to us we called on him. I narrated the entire incident and humbly requested him for his support. We furnished him the list of lost instruments and their respective amounts. We also gave him a letter, undertaking that any loss suffered would be our responsibility. This letter was given by me to the Branch Manager

LIC to raise their confidence and his comfort level. We also told him that we would credit the proceeds of all the 40 cheques/DDs next day as per usual clearing house norms, so that there would not be any expiry of the underlying Life Policies. LIC BM's approach was extremely supportive. He took our letter and as requested agreed to give us 40 letters signed by him in favour of the policy holders to issue duplicate cheques/DDs. He further gave us assurance that he would furnish the list of the related agents of the insurers, their addresses and telephone numbers. He further confirmed his personal support. We were overwhelmed by such a wonderful response and for which I am thankful to him forever. Our moral boosted because of his backing. The other two cheques worth of Rs 4 lakhs were issued by their local Divisional Office for internal transfer of funds. He informed us that on receiving conformation of nonpayment and record of stop payment from the concerned bank, he would manage the duplicate cheques himself. The Manager called us next day to collect all the information.

During the evening meeting of the day these positive developments were shared.

Next morning we again visited LIC. The Manager had kept all the information ready as per his words and had contacted some of his agents on our behalf.

Now our job was to contact all the 40 drawers of the cheques/DDs, give them our letter about loss and indemnity if required, confirmation from the branch bank about stop payment, letter from LIC to issue duplicate cheques. The task was formidable; however it was to be attended. At least we got something in our hand to proceed.

Our other two teams were also engaged. They had each contacted three to four branches handling the clearing of the different banks and could record the stop payment of the cheques / DDs. They were successful in obtaining the details of the drawers of few instruments. They collected the details of other branches of these banks on which the cheques were drawn. The next step was to visit these branches and seek details of the drawer in order to collect the duplicate of the cheques.

In the mean time, I contacted our Mumbai QCC center and requested them that the fate i.e realization of their high value cheques may require additional 3 to 4 days than usual 3 days. Those were five cheques but amount involved was Rs 95 lakhs. These cheques were issued by the clients of two different banks. We promptly recorded the stop payment and issued caution notice at these branches.

Let me give a gist of my conversation which took place with one of the Branch Managers. We called on the Bank Manager and after formal introduction I proceeded, 'Sir, I want your help. Unfortunately we had lost a bunch of cheques and two cheques were issued by your clients. Will you help us to meet the client? Please furnish his name and address so that we could contact him. In the mean time please record the caution in respect of these cheques. Sir, we will be obliged if you give a letter having stopped payment and noting caution or you may endorse the fact on our letter. May we also request you to telephone your client to help us?'

The usual questions raised were, 'How so many cheques could be misplaced? What action have you taken against the staff? Have you checked all the drawers and cupboards? Why the cheques were not stored in the safe? How you are going to obtain payments thereof? How will you face your customers? Can you come tomorrow as I am busy?' so on and so forth. But all these questions were contemplated by us and were answered in a very polite manner as practiced earlier. We had also decided to pursue and get the requisite information from the branches in one visit only to save time.

The clerical staff working with our branch had very good social status and contacts with staff of other banks and the people in general. We got immense help from the staff of the other banks to establish contacts with the customers of those branches in respect of lost cheques. Sometimes even the staff of other bank accompanied us to their customers. I had no words to thank them.

I vividly remember that even sub staff from our branch knew the Branch Managers of two Cooperative banks and their relationship was leveraged to reach to the drawer of the cheques.

Next day, I met the Divisional Manager of LIC. He had the knowledge about the loss of cheques and on briefing him the steps taken by us, he heartily appreciated the stand taken by us. He himself handed over two duplicate cheques amounting to Rs 4 lakhs and assured full support in case of any difficulty. We went to the branch in a very happy mood as there was a fruitful beginning of the task ahead. I still remember the glow in the eyes of the lady staff after looking at those cheques.

Our 5 to 6 clients who had deposited the cheques in their Savings/Current account came up themselves and brought duplicate cheques after knowing the whole episode. I would be obliged to them forever.

Having obtained all the basic information we started approaching the drawers of the cheques. There were several people who gave duplicate cheques to us on the basis of the stop payment letter of their bank. This was our experience in most of the cheques favouring LIC as they were backed by LIC letter and telephone call from their Insurance agent. We could collect about 15 duplicate cheques in a week and further 20 cheques in a fortnight. This had reduced the burden on us so far as numbers of instruments were concerned.

In some cases, we faced a lot of embarrassing questions, 'How does a bank looses cheques? Are you that negligent? How can we trust you? Why we should give duplicate cheques? Have you taken action against the staff? What security we had if banks are so negligent?' and so on.

We had anticipated all those questions and we had rehearsed the way in which those questions will be answered. All the staff was trained to listen to such questions keenly and answer them calmly; and assure them that we had taken suitable steps to avoid such a situation in future. It was also decided to request and pursue our goal of obtaining the duplicate cheques with perseverance.

In this way we were able to collect successfully about 70 numbers of duplicate cheques in period of about two months.

However in respect of few instruments we had special experiences which are enumerated below.

1) We were informed by the Bank 'S' that three cheques amounting to Rs.60 lakhs were issued by their client M/S MSN, who was the wholesaler of Hindustan Lever Limited (now Hindustan Unilever). These cheques were high value cheques sent for collection by QCC Mumbai. The BM also gave the letter about stop payment and address of the client. We called on Mr. Anil of M/S MSN and explained what had happened and requested for giving duplicate cheques. He laughed at us and plainly refused and asked further, 'Whether we want to close down his business' and emphatically said 'no'. Then we had to use our last straw, we told him, 'Sir, the concerned lady employee was employed on the compassionate grounds and had a daughter who is physically challenged and hence we request you to help us to support her otherwise an action against her is imminent.' This had softened his stand as reflected from his body language. He then asked us to show confirmation of stop payment from his Bank. It was shown to him.' I desired to help you people, but it is practically not possible as the Company may discontinue our credit facility,' he explained, 'The Company supplies goods on credit to us against the blank cheques sent in advance which they lodge with their Bank at Mumbai on due dates. And hence the Cheques with the same serial numbers must be honoured and get reflected in our statement of account, otherwise our credit facilities against cheques would be discontinued and we cannot afford it in any case.' He was very adamant. We requested, 'Sir, is there any authority who can permit the replacement of cheques as a special case?' He did not reply, but was definitely thinking. We were waiting very anxiously. He came out, 'I am not sure but the Sales Manager located at the Companies Regional Sales Office at Akola, located about 400 Kms. away, may help you in this matter. His name is Mr. Ramesh'. I requested for allowing his telephone (Mobiles

were very rare then). I telephoned our branch at Akola and called for Mr. D, who was a resourceful person, known to me because of my previous position as a faculty. I explained everything to him in a shortest possible way and asked whether he had any contacts with HLL. He assured me to come back within 10 minutes. The telephone rang and yes, he had spoken with Mr. Ramesh who agreed to listen to our case. I thanked and hung up. The next telephone was obviously to Mr. Ramesh, I explained everything to him and requested him to permit the replacement of the cheques. He agreed, I thanked him and again requested him to speak with Mr. Anil of M/S MSN and confirm to him. I further told him that I may need his help again. He heartily welcomed. Thus the matter was straightened up. Mr. Anil telephoned to his bank and confirmed about the nonpayment of the cheques. Then Mr. Anil gave us the prized three duplicate cheques amounting to Rs.60 lakhs. We thanked Mr. Anil and ran to the bank 'S' and against the cheques obtained Pay Order (now commonly known as Bankers' Cheque) for Rs. 60 lakhs from the S Bank. We expressed our gratitude to the Branch Manager for his support. Earlier Mr. Anil expressed his desire to visit the branch in two/ three days.

Mr. Anil was so pleased with our handling of the situation that he transferred his account to us and today he is the High Net Worth customer of the branch. He said 'If you are taking such a keen interest in the well being of your employees, I am sure your branch must be extending excellent service and caring the customers.'

2) The next target was to get the duplicate of remaining three QCC cheques amounting to Rs 34 lakhs. We found that these cheques were of DCB Bank. We called on the Manager of the Bank. He informed us that he was well acquainted with Mr. Wani, our Assistant Regional Manager. It was a very useful information and hence we telephoned him from there only. Mr. Wani knew about the loss of cheques and he

requested his Branch Manager friend to help us. On verification, it came to knowledge that both the cheques were issued by a single client and were in favour of Hindustan Lever Limited. The BM called the partner of the firm Mr. Kadir and requested, rather directed to issue the duplicate cheques. The same problem was again raised by Mr. Kadir, but now we had previous experience. Here also Mr. Ramesh of HLL came to our rescue; and Mr.Kadir issued the duplicate cheques. But now another problem cropped up that the account was already overdrawn. However as a special case the DCB Manager took the permission from his Head Office and the cheques were paid. We obtained the Pay Order for Rs 34 lakhs and were relived. We did not forget to communicate our thanks to DCB Manager, Mr. Ramesh, Mr. Kadir and our ARM for their help we could not have realized such a huge sum so quickly. Though, slightly off schedule, we had obtained the payments of QCC cheques and others amounting to around Rs.100 lakhs, thereby realization of the major amount out of the total sum involved.

I was regularly reporting the matter to The Regional Manager about the progress and he shown his satisfaction and also his full backing. All these efforts took over three weeks time. But surely our moral was very high as we were successful to a large extent.

3) We then focused on the DDs issued by the Cooperative Banks. Our SS team had undertaken this responsibility. They moved to the DD issuing branches in the district along with letter of caution from DD paying branches of The Cooperative Bank and the team collected all 10 duplicate Drafts. This was possible because of sheer good relations my local staff had with the people and their acquaintances. The proceeds were credited to the relevant accounts.

4) Three to four cheques were issued by Treasury. The drawee Bank was State Bank of Hyderabad. We had some tough time to record the stop payment instructions and to obtain

a letter in favour of the Treasury. But here also the contacts of our staff and their relationship with the Union Leaders of SBH were leveraged to get the necessary letter. One of our staff members was having close relationship with the Sub Treasury Officer. He then did manage the duplicate cheques thereof.

The other team through their persuasion could obtain several duplicate cheques. On our request the Branch Managers of two Nationalized Banks arranged for Duplicate DDs from their issuing branches themselves.

5) There were 2 DDs issued by BOB and they wanted the Indemnity from purchaser of the DDs. We were informed that the purchaser of the DDs was The Assistant Director of UGC Pune. As I was having several contacts at Pune, I took the responsibility. I moved through my friend in BOB, obtained a letter of caution, nonpayment and a format of the Indemnity for duplicate demand drafts from the concerned branch of BOB. My experience with UGC authority was wonderful as they cooperated with me and without hitch I could obtain the necessary Indemnity signed. Then obtaining the DDs was a cake walk. My belief that there are many kind and reasonable human beings in this world got substantiated.

6) Out of the lost 81 cheques, a cheque deposited by Insurance Company towards Group Insurance was very vital. When we visited the drawee Bank we understood that it was issued by a Sugar Factory and their account was not very satisfactory. The cheque for Rs 14 lakhs was issued towards the Group Insurance of the employees of the factory and was a must to be realized. The Manager of the Cooperative Bank was not sure that under the normal circumstances also he would have honoured the cheque. We had decided then to personally visit the Sugar factory which was located at a distance of about 90 Kms. We reached the factory at about 6 pm and found that the MD was out for some official work and would return at around 9 pm. We waited for him.

After his return we had dinner and spoke about the duplicate cheque. He entertained us well as Mr. Medhe, MD of another Sugar Mill, having account with us had telephoned him. He told us that we would tackle this matter tomorrow morning. We met next morning at around 9.30 am, had a breakfast with him and opened the subject. Though he appreciated the cause he was not sure about issuing duplicate, perhaps knowing that the cheque may not be honoured. We suggested him to issue a cheque on SBI branch located in the village. He agreed to give a cheque on local SBI for Rs10 lakhs. We accepted his proposal and requested him to arrange Rs 2 lakhs from some other account or give us cash. He gave us local SBI cheque and cash of Rs.2 lakhs. We appreciated for the help, thanked him and went to SBI branch. It was a village branch and BM was opening the branch. We waited for him, introduced ourselves and also told him about the loss of cheques. He asked 'what is the name of your staff?' We informed the name. Surprisingly he was quite sympathetic. We produced the cheque given by MD to us, 'Sir, on passing this cheque the account is overdrawn slightly, however I am taking the risk' said BM. We requested him to give us a consolidated DD for the cheque and the cash, which he agreed and deducted only nominal commission and DD was in our hand. We felt very fortunate that the difficult problem was solved very easily in an unexpected way. We thanked the BM and left. Afterwards we understood that the BM of SBI and the demised husband of our staff member were classmates.

7) We were not getting response in respect of two cheques in favour of LIC. In fact our team members visited twice but without any headway. One afternoon me and my colleague called on a businessman at a small shop. Only after several requests, he reveled that the cheques were not drawn by him but by his brother Mr. Ibrahim, staying in Dubai and he could not help rather he was worried because of the loss of cheques. We requested him to give contact number of

Mr. Ibrahim and to accompany us to a nearby STD/ISD booth. He told us to wait for about half an hour as Mr. Ibrahim must be offering 'Namaz' at this time. We telephoned after an hour. I introduced myself with 'Salam Alekum, Insha Allaha' and repeated the whole story. He must be in the praying mood and hence asked us to give the receiver to his brother Mr. Jameel. They spoke and Mr. Ibrahim agreed to give a single cheque instead of two cheques as he had only one signed cheque. We thanked and left. Thus we got realization of all the cheques in favour of LIC in about one and half month's period.

8) Thus we had successfully obtained the duplicate of all the 79 cheques in the record time of about two and half months. However still we were struggling to obtain duplicate of last two cheques numbered 80 and 81 each for Rs1,10,220/- out of the lost bunch. These instruments were sent to us in collection by our Aurangabad Branch and were the proceeds of National Savings Certificates issued by the local Post Office. We had visited the Post Office at least thrice but the concerned Post Master dismissed us by saying that it is not possible. During our fourth visit the relevant Clerk handling NSC, told us that the concerned Post Master would be retiring in next two months and hence we should meet the other Post Master, who reports during the evening time. We did meet him but he also told us that there was no procedure to issue duplicate cheques. The relevant NSC handling Clerk informed that we should meet the Assistant Post Master General and seek his guidance. Next day we visited him, but he was also not sure and directed us to go to the Auditor located elsewhere in the town. On contacting the Auditor, we were informed that he had to look into the Rule Book. We had earlier met the Treasury Officer and he had shown from the Rule Book the procedure to be followed under such circumstances. We had accordingly recorded the stop payment of those cheques in the books at SBH and also obtained a letter from them to that effect. The Auditor

referred the Rule Book and informed us the procedure. He also gave a certified copy of the procedure. We revisited the Post Office and gave the copy to the Post Master. He took it with great reluctance and told that he would require an independent letter from SBH. The clerk silently prepared the letter and gave it to us. We went back to SBH there we faced wrath of the dealing officer, but we successfully obtained the relevant letter for the Post Office. All these papers were then sent to Assistant Post Master General for his approval. He did respond quickly after going through the Rule Book and gave his approval letter to us. The letter was handed over to the second shift Post Master and ultimately we got the duplicate of the last two Cheques, **Numbered 80 and 81** after a period of about three months. On reaching the branch, memorable jubilation and celebration took place. Every staff member felt greatly relieved and a smile of satisfaction was reflecting on every body's face.

It was the first night after three months that I could sleep peacefully.

Although we had to pass through many trying days, we were successful in our endeavour with flying colours. Because of this episode, I came in contact with around 250 people right from The Divisional Manager of LIC, three whole sellers of HLL, many Agents of LIC, several small traders, Authorities related with Post Office, 25 Bankers to many individuals. Observing our approach towards the problem the people were attracted towards our Bank and through the contacts we added the Cash Credit accounts of 2 whole sellers of HLL, three Current accounts and at least 50 to 60 Savings Bank accounts. Additionally we could convert our relationship to garner several Housing Loan and Personal loan accounts.

Take Away :

➢ **The mammoth task of obtaining 81 duplicate cheques for Rs112.50 lakhs in a record period of three months** was possible because of the dedicated efforts, persuasion, planning and of course the team work of the staff members.

➢ Not only the difficult task of obtaining duplicate cheques was handled professionally but also it provided a practical example of how an adversity was successfully converted into the business opportunity for the Bank.

➢ **Characteristics of a Team**
- Team should set clear and important goals.
- Team structure should be result driven.
- Members should be committed. They should collaborate freely.
- Teams should have principled leadership.
- Leadership responsibility should be shared.
- Collective efforts are stronger than the individual.
- Teams work with other groups and systems.
- Members talk about, and agree upon how the team will operate.
- Goals established are discussed and the team plans how to meet them.
- Members can express their feelings and ideas.
- Boundaries are identified and discussed.
- Disagreements are constructively addressed.
- Everybody contributes to the work of the team.
- People are responsible for leading when needed; people follow and stand in support of the leader.
- Synergy should be the ultimate goal of any group to achieve the target.
- Working in teams provides the organization and its employees both tangible and intangible benefits.

• • •

(2) 'The Feather in the Cap'

It was an afternoon of a humid day in June 2010. I was busy preparing the visit report when the phone started ringing I answered and got quickly attentive as it was from the Secretariat department of Chairman and Managing Director. Sir, 'Good Noon, this is Gokhale speaking.' Our esteemed CMD was on the line and he informed me that he would like to post me at our bank's main branch Mumbai Main Office as the bank would be celebrating the Year Dec 2010 to Dec 2011 as **The Centenary Year** and as a sequel to it the Grand Old Building of MMO was to be fully renovated. This being a task in itself he wanted that I should handle this. I may add that there was no major renovation undertaken for last 40 to 50 years and several earlier attempts were not fully successful as there were many hurdles.

I received my transfer orders from Rajkot to Mumbai Main Office and joined in the last week of June 2010. There were several meetings between AGM, GAD, CO; Mr. Ajay Vyas and his staff, myself, the Contractor and an architect during the period from 10th July to 10th August. The Contractor desired that we should vacate the entire 1st floor premises of the branch.

To understand the enormous work involved I must state that the **'Monumental Heritage Building' of the Bank comprises of 7 floors and the two basements.** While the outside façade was to be kept untouched as per Heritage Act, the inside was to undergo repairs and total facelift / changes. The area of each floor was more than 8400 Sq. feet. At one time the MMO was the biggest branch in Asia and around 2000 personnel were working in that building.

When I took charge of MMO the staff strength was strong 185 (Officers-45, Clarks 70, Sub staff- 70). Out of these the ladies staff was around 65.There were 125 work stations engaged by CTO'S and Officer Staff, 3 Servers and 3 UPS / Battery units. Similarly the branch had CBS system, 3 other systems for connectivity with RBI for Currency chest, Government Tax

Collection and SWIFT for Forex Transactions. There were 12 to 15 very heavy Cash Safes and about 100 Cub-boards meant for storing the voluminous Paper Records, Registers, Vouchers, Challans, Ledgers, Loan documents etc. There were total 15 to 18 departments like Current, Savings, Fixed deposits; Loans, Cash Credit, Forex, GAD, Govt., Personnel, Cash departments and others. There were two huge cabins of app.1000 sq. feet each one for Branch Manager and other an old board room. There were old fashioned counters numbering around 60, 75 tables, chairs and 25 air conditioners fixed in the windows. All these things were housed on the ground floor which would be totally refurbished right from changing the flooring. There were Union offices on the floor which had to be shifted. In order to start work and finish it off before 15th May 2011, so that the inauguration of the renovated MMO, proposed on 31st May would match with **The Centenary Celebration Year of The Bank commencing on 21st December 2010 and culminating on 21st December 2011.**

The various contractors expressed their anxiety to get the entire floor vacant by 15th of August 2010, so that they would get a period of exactly nine months to finish the entire herculean task. The major work to be undertaken was 1) To completely dismantle the existing furniture and fixture, all electrical fittings, remove the POP false ceiling, all windows with AC to be refurbished and also to remove the floor tiles. 2) To redo the entire interior from floor to ceiling to its original palatial height of 15 feet. 3) To restore all 30 odd columns to its original ornamental glory. 4) To fix centralized AC 5) Data cabling for 100 odd work stations 6) Electrification to match with the proposed furniture, fixture and interiors 8) Telephone Cabling 8) To renovate the exterior façade in tune with the permission granted under The Heritage Act and to restore it to its past glory etc. The list given above was to understand the complexity of the job and coordination required with all agencies and CO.

The task that was to be handled by The Team MMO was to close down the existing branch, shift the entire branch lock stock and barrel in the adjacent building also owned by the bank and on finishing the renovation of main building to restart branch there. The crux was that the premises to be occupied for the temporary period had a sitting arrangement that is counters and tables for 60 odd staff. This hall was housing only the Savings Department of the branch some 10 years back. There were no computer terminals and building was not used for those many years.

We had three/four unions in the bank and the branch was a strong hold because of its staff strength. I remember when I spoke casually with the leaders they had a laugh and one of them commented that even a strong BM like Mr. XXX failed in this endeavour and others had also failed.

It was a real challenge to surmount all these odds. I had to think and prepare a strategy and a suitable plan and then toughest part of it was to execute it. The time available with me was a constraint and another aspect which was tougher than this was to make a suitable ground that the staff would be with me to support and accept the proposed changes. In order to communicate with people and make the changes palatable, I proposed to hold three to four meetings.

During the first meeting, it was decided that Chief Manager who was working with the branch for over two and half years would begin, prepare some soft turf for me to sow seeds. But he miserably failed and then I had to take over. In first few sentences I informed about various preparations which were going on at CO for the ensuing **Centenary function** of the Bank and further told that bank had **invited** all of us to be a part of that Memorable function which would be enjoyed by only few of us, as such occasions happen only once in the **life time**. Our CMD has bestowed the responsibility on us to complete the renovation of the '**Monumental Heritage Building** 'of the Bank i.e. our **MMO** as a part of the **Centenary Celebration. I appeal** to all of you to contribute your mite. These words did play the trick and I could see the acceptance on the faces of most of them. Having sown the seeds of inclusiveness, I further assured them that we will be soon occupying a place with great ambiance, fully air conditioned branch and with all updated systems. We would be working in a very soothing, totally hygienic and a very delightful ultra modern branch than the present one. We concluded on a very positive note, having accepted the challenge.

The next meeting followed after a gap of about 7 days, as I had to plan the other things. Along with an experienced GAD officer Mr. Ganesh Patil and a young energetic IT officer Shri Shashank Kumbhare, I had already visited the other premises and appointed a labour contractor for cleaning the premises. These premises were not in use for over 7 years. A contractor was also assigned the job of completing the requisite data cabling and electrification work. Of course, I had elaborately deliberated with these two confederates on various related issues and consciously chalked out the plan of action.

During the second meeting I communicated with all the staff members that we would have to vacate the present premises and shift it to the next building. I opened up all my cards and very honestly in plain words explained the details of the renovation work to be done and how there was no alternative other than to vacate. That was a sour pill but while prescribing, it was very well wrapped with a sugar coat. I also asked the experiences of the two staff members who had recently renovated their own houses. Both of them spoke very well stating that initially they suffered a lot but very happy, peaceful and satisfied they are in their excellent new dwelling. Since the experience was from their own colleagues the acceptance was total. I convinced them that we will have to face similar problems for about 8 to 9 months but those would be the pranks of the new birth. The fact of change and the acceptance thereof sunk in them slowly but firmly.

Simultaneously I was in a continuous contact with the union stake holders. Although they were not so much convinced about success of the renovation plan, they assured their full support to me and also agreed to communicate this from their platform. Perhaps this was the result of their declaration of unstinted support to the management for The Centenary Function. Besides this the other reason was that in my earlier stint at CO as CM, CSD, I had helped most of them and earned a good name and respect from all the unions.

The third meeting was for action and fixing the time table. We had floated small committees of 3 to 4 persons and assigned different tasks, besides this each department had individual Captains for solving problems of their own department. This was essential as each department had 8 to 12 staff members and equal number of store-wells per department for safe keeping of the documents. It was clarified that each department would get only 3 cub-boards at their work place and others would be kept in a temporary godown on 2nd floor of the building. The captain in consultation with other staff of the department would decide what registers, ledgers and document would be kept at work station for that department. It was decided to put the identification numbers on all the cub-boards in a particular way as suggested by one of the daftaries. It was also decided that it would be the responsibility of the CTO and Officer to number and shift their PC Monitor, server, key board, mouse and its printers. Though this appears to be a simple task, but after taking into consideration the total work stations numbered 110, one can understand its complexity. And yes the human affinity with the computers, key board, mouse and others. Two other daftaries took the responsibility of shifting all cub-boards and arranging in the proposed Godown as well to control it. The energy level was so high that two officers, two clarks and two sub staffs took initiatives to help any department requiring support.

The GAD subcommittee assigned the place to be occupied in the makeshift building. We observed that still we would need more space for our Loan, Credit, Documentation, Recovery, Government Transactions, Forex and Inward/Outward departments with about 25 work stations. As per suggestions from our second CM we shifted these departments on 2nd floor under his command. We had to make all provisions for those number of work stations. We had a daunting task of shifting two Servers and two UPS with Battery Units in the make shift place and the third one on 2nd floor and to connect all these in a LAN, apart from those on the two basement sights of Currency Chest and Safe Deposit Lockers. Thus data cables and telephone cables had to be connected across the road between the two buildings. This impossible task at **Mumbai** was managed by Shri Ganesh Patil, for which he deserves a special mention.

One lady officer and one GAD officer accepted the challenge of maintaining the housekeeping and hygiene at the branch. In the premises there was only one wash room and it was agreed that it would be reserved for ladies only. The gents would utilize the facilities in adjoining building of the Bank for which they had to traverse around 100 meters. It was a rare and exemplary comradeship shown by the staff of MMO and I salute them for their dedication.

It was not that all the travel was very smooth; there were always several stumbling blocks in the journey. The work stations selected by the GAD for 2 departments were not acceptable as the area was very small; some departments wanted at least 5 cub-boards instead of 3; one department occupied a place not meant for them; some departments wanted additional electrical points; some officers complained about the chairs provided and so on and so forth. There was no arrangement for storing of drinking water and water for the wash room since the premises were not used for several years. Then two Sintex tanks, water coolers with filter, a wash basin and requisite taps were fixed. However all problems were resolved in the best possible manner, either by discussion or some time even by little force when there were no alternatives. I introduced the concept of **Just in Time,** which was common in many industrial units for management of the input, to reduction of inventory. In our case it was only management of necessary documents for a week.

The proceedings in respect of all the committee meetings held were properly recorded including the names of captains, the authority given to them, work to be attended, the progress and the expenditure allowed by them for various jobs, and even the payments made to contractors. One of our Chief Managers, a task master had taken this responsibility and was attending the job seriously. This had helped us to complete the task in time and management of expenses.

Having completed all the ground work to the best possible extent and after testing the connectivity for working of CBS and other computer systems we had decided on a Wednesday to shift to the proposed temporary premises from next Saturday. The team led by an officer requested all the lady staff members that they should bring the cloth bags from their residence to fill in the articles in their drawers and shift those to their destination drawers. On the decided Saturday as notified to the customers for last several days we closed down the business exactly at 12.30 pm and the staff as directed started shifting the documents, ledgers and registers in a quite disciplined manner. One group was engaged in closure of accounts, cash and day end activities, as the system was to be disconnected. Earlier, through the appointed labour contractor we had moved about 60 odd cub boards, with proper numbering, to the make shift building at specific places. This was a daunting task as those Godrej cub-boards were very heavy and some had documents inside. An equal number of cub boards were shifted to the 2nd and 3rd floors where we had occupied three halls, two for work stations and two as godowns to keep the cub-boards.

The most important and vital job had now begun dismantling, shifting and reconnecting the computer systems, 2 UPS units and battery units. In all 85 units were installed in the next building, 20 units on 2nd and 3rd floors of the existing building and remaining 5 work stations in the two departments located in the basement of the old building. All these units were connected in a LAN. I had no words to praise our vendors. IT officer Shri Shashank who was instrumental in successfully achieving this formidable task and that too without many hiccups. Of course it took us around 8 to 10 hours of marathon working, but all of us left that Saturday with great satisfaction.

On Monday Shri Shashank started the System with a thumping heart, but all went well except two three systems which started after repairing. The working started quite normally with little bit grumbling from the clients for the inconvenience, but our staff handled it well. There were some problems, difficulties, complaints from the customers and even from some of the staff members during the next 8 months of working, but somehow we were able to surmount those with the support received from the Higher Management, Union Leaders and of course the wonderful customers who patiently accepted the change. My thanks are due to them!

The very important job of renovating **The Heritage Building** and to restore it to its past glory, and at the same time to make all the modern architecture available in it was the tumultuous task to be completed from various contractors within the stipulated time frame. It was carried out by the team from GAD, Central Office in a very professional manner, under the leadership of Mr. Ajay Vyas and his team members Mr. Vijay Saxsena and Mr. Mistry, who had also substantial contribution. I owe a lot to all of them for their efforts.

The renovation was completed in record time of about 8 months and again there was time for shifting to the Grand Old Premises. While the renovation was going on there were several hurdles in the Data Cabling, repairing the lift and fixing the AC plant etc but all the difficulties were overcome. We again decided to shift on Saturday to the newly renovated building. Again we had to repeat the entire drill which we had done 8-9 months back. Since we had done the earlier drill in a systematic way, this time it was much easier. Again Mr. Shashank along with the vendors did the job of shifting and again starting all the computers in the same professional way. Staff was very happy with the ambiance and the friendly environment and well lit beautiful premises. Of course there also we did face certain problems which were fixed without many difficulties. Our customers were equally happy with the large and cozy sitting arrangement and facilities provided to them. The staff was contented as they received all the facilities which were assured to them.

On 31st May 2011, the scheduled day the Grand

Inauguration Function was arranged. The Chief Guest of the function was The Municipal Commissioner of Greater Mumbai, Mr. Subodh Kumar. The function was presided over by our esteemed CMD Shri Shridhar. For the function we had invited the relatives from the family of our beloved founder Sir Sorabji Pochkhanawala and the renowned clients from the house of Tatas, Godraj, Videocon and many others. All the other executives and dignitaries and all the staff were also invited. One and all appreciated the efforts taken by the staff without their co-operation this glorious day would not have dawned. While extending the vote of thanks, I specially requested our esteemed CMD to felicitate all the major contributing persons. They were our house keeping contractor, electrical contractor; the architect and contractor of the beautifully renovated historic building. The Best Working Officer of the Year Mrs. Monica, best Clerk Mrs. Vrunda and the Best Sub Staff worker Mr.Tanaji were felicitated along with Mr. Shashank Kumbhare our IT Officer for his exemplary contribution.

I must mention here that the Branch Manager's cabin which was once adored by Our Banks' Founder Sir Sorabji Pochkhanawalla was converted into a Beautiful Museum after restoring it to its past glory. Similarly the Old Board Room was also restored with all its heritage architecture and old invaluable artifacts.

I am extremely satisfied and feel myself honoured by the rare of the rarest opportunity showered on me by the bank to undertake the renovation of the *'Monumental Heritage Building' of the Bank during The Centenary Year 2010-2011. I had also the enviable honour to occupy the revered chair of our Founder and I am the last Branch Manager to be bestowed with such kind of honour. What other honour one can expect from his Institution!*

I had also one more feather in my cap that during the renovation I could lay my hands on 'The Minuets of The First Board Meeting of The Bank, held in 1911' and this is a Historic Document.

Take Away :

The skills one requires to complete the tumultus tasks are-

I) **Motivation**
- ➢ The satisfaction of need of inclusion is an important motivator to the staff.
- ➢ **Compelling Communication**
  Put your points in persuasive, clear ways so that people are motivated. They should be also clear about expectations of the management.

II) **For Working in a Team**
- ➢ Get to know one another.
- ➢ Establish consensus as to team's purpose.
- ➢ Identify available resources.
- ➢ Establish rules of behaviour.

III) **Time Management**
'If you Fail to Plan, you Plan to Fail.' – Anonymous
'For every minute spent in organizing, an hour is earned.' – Anonymous
- ➢ Believe it is possible to get more out of available time.
- ➢ Writing down goals is the first important step.
- ➢ Break down goals to tasks.
- ➢ Understand your 'most effective time zone'.
- ➢ Create daily TO DO List for next 3 months.
- ➢ Prioritize and schedule the tasks.
- ➢ Create processes on most of the tasks.
- ➢ Invest time to train someone and delegate in steps.
- ➢ Leave the habit of attending to everything that comes in front.

IV) **Delegation**
- ➢ Have faith that the other person can do it.
- ➢ Convey expectations, rules and processes.

> Observe in the beginning, Correct when necessary and encourage.
> Be keen to help someone and spread interdependence.
> Be sure that you are not the weak link of the chain.

• • •

3) Some Handy Management Tips

(a) A perfectionist attitude of a Manager Mr. 'I'.

I use to handle all the work myself as I had an understanding / misnomer that I am the only who understands and could handle the job perfectly. Everything should be done in a way I desire and thought that, if the work is assignment to someone he many not understand properly and will not give justice to the job.

Later It dawned on me that I could attend the work to certain extent only, as such it was imperative that I should share it with someone. This means delegation. Most important aspects of delegation are :

1) We should choose proper persons who can effectively handle the job to be delegated.

2) Secondly they should be given the full knowledge about the job to be undertaken; otherwise they will make several mistakes, for which they would not be responsible but you will be. You should not blame them in fact it was you who had mistaken.

3) Having chosen the proper persons fit to handle the job; then keep them fully informed about the work they have to handle, give them the training and skill to efficiently undertake the assigned work.

4) Once the work is assigned it is necessary to give them sufficient time and not to monitor continuously on micro management i.e. over the shoulders or with one eye always on them.

If you micro manage as you are not confident whether the work would be attended perfectly as per your standards, would only result into 'you knowing the assigned job perfectly'. Of course this would be a waste of time of not only you, but also of the company. Remember the constant micro management always proves to be a stumbling block in the development of the personnel who are working for you. Then even for a very minor decision they will look towards you; as they will be fearful in even minor decision making and will be only your obedient labourers. As such those of your subordinates who are wishing to go upscale in their career will feel you are a stumbling block. Hence remember you should never sniff over the shoulders.

In the words of Management Guru PETER DRUCKER

'One must remember that when proper people are selected, given all the information and as well the necessary knowledge, training and skills one must give them sufficient freedom to work and should not micromanage them. Of course you should not reach the other end i.e. not to take the interim reviews. Otherwise at the end of the project it may so happen that you may understand that the entire project has gone fut, and you could not do anything, but loose the customer.'

So Management By Objectives *means not only Delegation but surely monitoring the job so that Rectification or necessary changes can be done in time, of course it should not be Micro Managed.*

(b) Motivating People

In any Business remember ultimately the People matter. The first step is to select proper persons for the job, properly distribute the work amongst them, and give them the necessary training, skills and knowledge. Then you must encourage them while working; keep alive the enthusiasm for work. Help and support them while working; in case of difficulty work with them, be on their side when the situation demands. Have a feed back of the work for rectification if needed and lastly but surely Recognize/ Applaud/Praise/Say Well done/Gift them for the work they had performed. This is the crux of the Management.

(c) Staff Motivation to the Source

Families influence the employees and their well being in turn affects the employee's work life. This concept had been utilized effectively by the author while working in the branches in the following way.

- A meeting of the children aged 12 to 14 years of the staff members and customers were arranged addressed by the successful students who had availed Education Loan from Bank and studying at IIT's, NIT, MBA, MBBS Colleges and in Foreign Countries. Students explained how they prepared for Competitive Examinations for I I T, GRE etc and how they are at a foreign country. Sharing of their Experiences proved to be quite motivating.

- After crossing targets of the branch the spouses of the staff members were appreciated for the contribution of their better half.

- Bhajan and Geet programmes were arranged for parents of the staff members.

- When working as BM, CM, RM, AGM, DGM the Best Wishes were personally communicated to the wards of the staff appearing for 10th and 12th Standard.

- All meritorious students were felicitated.

- Personally visited the residence of the staff members and communicated with their parents and spouse for preparing for promotional examinations and for accepting elevation.

- Anniversary functions were arranged at all offices and family members were invariably invited. These programmes were of the people, by the people and for the people.

- In such programmes chance to different staff members assigning different responsibilities was given.

● ● ●

ACRONYMS USED

1 RO	Regional Office	21 RM	Regional Manager
2 ZO	Zonal Office	22 ZM	Zonal Manager
3 CO	Central Office	23 GM	General Manager
4 HO	Head Office	24 CMD	Chairman and Managing Director
5 BO	Branch Office	25 BM	Branch Manager
6 MMO	Mumbai Main Office	26 MD	Managing Director
7 DCO	Deputy Chief Officers	27 MF	Manifold
8 DRI	Differential Rate of Interest	28 RR	Railway Receipt
9 DD	Demand Draft	29 LR	Lorry Receipt
10 TT	Telegraphic Transfer	30 MTR	Motor Transport Receipt
11 BG	Bank Guarantee	31 BL	Bill of Lading
12 LC	Letter of Credit	32 UGC	University Grants Commission
13 HNW	High Net Worth	33 IIT	Indian Institute of Technology
14 RTGS	Real Time Gross Settlement	34 ZSTC	Zonal Staff Training Center
15 NEFT	Electronic Funds Transfer	35 PPT	Power Point Presentation
16 CBS	Centralized Banking Solution	36 GRE	Graduate Record Examination
17 CTO	Computer Terminal Operator	37 HNI	High Net worth Individual
18 LandT	Larson and Toubro	38 Forex - Foreign Exchange	
19 CSR	Corporate Social Responsibility	39 CRPF - Central Reserve Police Force	
20 AGM	Assistant General Manager		

DISCLAIMER *All information, including graphical representations, etc provided in this presentation is for exclusive use of the owner. No part of the document may be reproduced in any form or by any means, electronic or otherwise, without written permission of the owner/author.*

The Book describes the Real Life situations faced by a Banker. There are no intentions to harm anybody's emotions. The names of the Persons and Places appearing may be different from the Actual Names but the situations are all Real.

About the Author

Waman Gokhale

A Banking professional with 40 plus experience in Central Bank of India.

Banking Experience :

- Worked as Branch Head in all types and sizes of Branches right from Rural, Semi-Urban, Urban to Metro branches.
- Privilege of being a Branch Head of most Prestigious Branch of the Bank, Mumbai Main Branch during the CENTEINARY YEAR of the BANK.
- As an Administrator at Head Office for over 3 years where more than 2000 staff was working.
- Regional Head of Rajkot Region.
- **Last Assignment**
  Deputy General Manager/Chief Internal Auditor of Mumbai Audit Zone for **Central Bank of India**. Retired in August 2013.

Teaching Experience :

- Faculty for over 5 years in Zonal Staff Training Center, Pune of Central Bank of India.
- Guest Faculty in various Colleges in Pune and Mumbai like Modern College and Symbiosis College, etc.
- Guest Faculty in Training Colleges of PSU Banks, Sir Sorabaji Pochkhanawala Bankers' Training College, Mumbai, South Indian Bank's Staff Training College, Bangalore.
- Conducted several Tests for Recruitment of staff at all levels while working at Central Bank Of India.
- Acted as a Master Trainer for Globsyn Skills.
- Master Trainer on the panel of Indian Institute of Banking and Finance.

Key Achievements :

- Published E-book in 2012, 'A Kit On Documentation' Available online on Central Bank Of India for Staff Only Site.
- Panel Member on Saurashtra University as an Expert for deciding Curriculum for MBA students (2009-10).
- Mentored several persons in the Bank who are currently occupying Very Good positions.
- Helped lot of students for their presentations on various subjects related with Finance as well for preparing their Projects.

Educational Qualifications :

- Bachelor of Science from Nagpur University.
- Bachelor of Laws from Symbiosis College of Law, Pune University.
- Chartered Associate of Indian Institute of Bankers (CAIIB).
- Proficiency in Rajbhasha (IIB Certificate).

www.ingramcontent.com/pod-product-compliance
Lightning Source LLC
Chambersburg PA
CBHW070705280626
47159CB00022B/2092